AFRAID TO LOVE

Sue Anders is overjoyed to be flying to Kuala Lumpur in Malaysia to attend her pen friend's wedding. When she meets businessman David Blake, she responds to his charm, in spite of her determination not to become involved with him — or any man. Sue finds herself caught up in some dangerous business deals . . . and the outcome becomes a matter of life or death. Maybe she should have heeded her inner voice of caution?

KAREN ABBOTT

AFRAID TO LOVE

Complete and Unabridged

LINFORD
Leicester

First published in Great Britain in 2005

First Linford Edition
published 2006

British Library CIP Data

Abbott, Karen
    Afraid to love.—Large print ed.—
Linford romance library
    1. Romantic suspense novels
    2. Large type books
    I. Title
    823.9'14 [F]

    ISBN 1–84617–374–4

Published by
F. A. Thorpe (Publishing)
Anstey, Leicestershire

Set by Words & Graphics Ltd.
Anstey, Leicestershire
Printed and bound in Great Britain by
T. J. International Ltd., Padstow, Cornwall

This book is printed on acid-free paper

1

Sue Anders roused herself from the sense of drowsiness that enveloped her and tried to remember exactly where she was. Every muscle in her body seemed to be aching as the steady drone of high-powered engines forced itself into her consciousness.

She focussed her eyes on the flashing digital message that was running across the computer screen in front of her. It announced that the Boeing 747 jumbo jet would be landing at Kuala Lumpur International Airport in twenty minutes. It would be 7.45 a.m. local time.

Sue groped between her feet, grasping the handle of her small backpack, and excused herself as she squeezed past the passengers on her right. After almost thirteen hours in the air, she felt in need of a refreshing shower . . . but knew she would have to make do with simply washing her face and hands.

Ten minutes later, as she made her way back to her seat, her face shone with the thrill of expectancy, still hardly able to believe that in a few minutes time she would be landing in Malaysia.

The invitation to finally meet Amu, her Malaysian pen-friend, and attend her wedding, had offered her the chance in a lifetime and, with no prospects of going any further in her current job in the office of a local business, she had handed in her resignation, put her few possessions into storage in a colleague's attic and booked her return flight from Manchester to Kuala Lumpur with a local travel agent.

There was no-one to try to persuade her to do otherwise and no-one to wave her farewell . . . although her former colleagues had clubbed together to buy her a small travel-bag and had wished her the best of luck on her final Friday afternoon.

She knew she'd have to get another

job eventually . . . but, for the next few weeks, she was free to enjoy whatever came her way.

She glanced through the window, catching her breath as the aeroplane descended through the thin layer of white, wispy clouds that, from above, had seemed like a snow-covered plateau tinged with pink and apricot rays from the early morning sun. Now, it was a landscape of brilliant green, acre upon acre of what became apparent as tall palm trees fringing the coastline. Tiny terracotta-roofed buildings were dotted among them in orderly groups.

In the distance, she could pick out the twin Petronas Towers standing in the middle of the city . . . and there was the Telecom Tower, standing tall among the other skyscrapers. In the early-morning sunshine the effect was magnificent.

Sue felt a lump in her throat as she drank in the beauty below, watching entranced as the plane banked and ponderously turned towards the runway, rapidly losing height as they went.

The landing was smooth, almost an anti-climax, and Sue patiently took her place in line as the passengers disembarked in orderly fashion, collected her travel bag from the carousel and made her way towards the arrivals lounge.

Now, where was Amu? She had promised to be there if she possibly could.

Sue's brown eyes, alight with anticipation, skimmed the assortment of people waiting for relatives and friends off the aeroplane that was now taxiing away to be serviced. It was immediately clear that Amu wasn't there.

They had never met, but had exchanged photographs over the years. Sue held the image of a pretty, dark-skinned, dark-haired Malaysian girl in her mind.

Her face clouded for a moment. Amu had been raised in a local orphanage called The Sheepfold, where she had been abandoned as a small child, and it was to the orphanage that Sue had addressed her constant stream of letters over the years.

During the many years of friendship via letters and photographs, Amu had told of the sudden appearance of her aunt when she, Amu, was old enough to go out to work and earn money. Her Aunt Rathi claimed Amu as her only niece and removed her from the shelter of the orphanage into her own home.

After insisting that it was Amu's duty to work in order to provide her benefactress with a better standard of living, she took all of Amu's wage, giving only a pittance back to Amu for herself.

Reading between the lines, Sue suspected that Aunt Rathi wasn't pleased that Amu was to be married in a few weeks' time because it meant that she would lose control of Amu's wages. Sue pressed her lips together. She hoped Vishnu, Amu's fiancé, was strong enough to stand up to Aunt Rathi.

Shrugging away Amu's problems for the moment, Sue returned her thoughts to the one at hand. What should she do? The only answer was to take a taxi to the orphanage, the only address that she knew, for it was there that Sue was to stay for the period of her visit.

She spotted a notice on the wall by the exit, urging would-be clients to obtain their travel coupon before approaching the taxi rank.

Her enquiry set in motion a heated debate within the booking office, but eventually a consensus of opinion seemed to be reached and Sue handed over the required number of ringgits for her taxi coupon, hoping the agreed location was correct. Clutching her coupon, she headed purposely towards the exit.

She was tall and slender, with a graceful walk that a model would be proud of. Her long dark brown hair, that usually floated out behind her as she walked, clung to her head in the sudden blast of heat that hit her as she stepped outside.

Wow! She'd been told to expect it to

be hot . . . but this was something else! How did people cope with it? And to think that this was merely the heat of the early morning. What would the temperature be like by mid-day?

'You'll get used to it,' a masculine voice murmured at her side.

Even though Sue was tall, the voice came from above and she glanced upwards into a pair of dark grey eyes that seemed to sweep over her with a degree of admiration.

'I hope so! I'm here for six weeks.' Sue smiled.

'Good for you!' the man rejoined, his eyes already glancing along the road to where Sue could see a silver grey limousine pulling out of line. 'Enjoy your stay.'

She watched as he strode towards the elegant car with only a medium-sized piece of hand-luggage, mildly acknowledging the man's charisma . . . and somehow certain that he was being met by a woman.

The heat of the air was getting to her,

and Sue sank into the rear seat of the taxi, thankful that the air-conditioning was functioning. The four-lane highway was busy with commuter traffic, all of which seemed to be following their own version of the highway code . . . if there was one, Sue reflected doubtfully.

Vehicles changed lanes without signals having been made and shot off down side exits with no apparent lessening of speed. Other vehicles nosed their way into the flow of traffic, demanding that space be made, regardless of its likelihood.

She took her eyes off the traffic and sank into reflection of where she was going. It had been the one downside to her visit . . . that she was to stay at the orphanage. Although, to be fair, she acknowledged that Aunt Rathi could not be imposed upon. The apartment was small, according to Amu's description of it.

Would the orphanage be any better?

A vision of a tall, dark red brick, solid square building imposed itself upon

Sue's inner vision and she couldn't prevent a shudder that wracked her body.

'Grow up!' she demanded of herself. Amu had nothing but praise for the establishment that had nurtured her infancy. It would be all right.

Lost in thought, Sue was suddenly aware that the taxi had turned off the main highway on to a badly-kept single-track road. Plain concrete bungalows were on both sides of the track with the occasional two-storey dwelling amongst them. It was outside one of these that the taxi drew up and the driver leaped out of his seat to open the rear door.

Whilst the driver lifted out her wheeled suitcase, Sue scrambled out of the taxi and looked around at the motley assembly of buildings, wondering which one to approach. The heat was once more tremendous and, in a wave of homesickness, she wondered for the first time if her coming to Malaysia had been such a good idea after all.

Before the thought had had time to take root, she realised that the driver was looking at her expectantly as he held out the handle of her suitcase towards her. Of course! He'd be expecting a tip. She had opened her purse and took out a couple of blue one-ringgit notes.

The driver bowed as he thanked her and pointed to one of the two-storey buildings. 'You go through that door, missy,' he said, nodding and smiling at the same time. 'You go up stairs. He very nice man.'

Sue smiled her thanks and took hold of her case, aware that her stomach was churning. It was a different time, a different place . . . but the memory was still the same.

'Go through that door and up the stairs,' the command had been, 'and don't forget to mind your manners and say 'please' and 'thank you'!'

Thrusting the memory away with a determined toss of her head, Sue approached the doorway, dragging her suitcase behind her. The white paint was peeling off the open door and frame, probably due to the constant heat that beat upon it, she thought.

Clustered in the small square hall-way, not much wider than the door itself, was a pair of shoes, and Sue remembered what Amu had told her about the local custom of removing outdoor footwear before entering people's homes. As she eased off her sandals, she noticed the poor quality of the worn stair carpet and wondered afresh what was before her for the next few weeks. Could she cope? Could she bear it?

Grimacing with determination, she hauled her suitcase up the stairs and pushed open the door at the top. Immediately, she found herself in a small office, with clean painted walls, a few bookcases and a desk, where a pretty Malaysian girl was seated.

The girl looked up and smiled. 'May I help you?' she asked in perfect English.

Sue smiled back, a little shakily. 'Hello. I'm Sue Anders, Amu Ngoh's friend. I was . . . er . . . expecting her to meet me at the airport but she wasn't there.' She hesitated slightly before adding, 'I'm looking for the pastor who is in charge here. I think I'm to stay here for a few weeks.'

The girl beamed, rising from her seat and coming to the front of the desk. 'Oh, welcome, Sue. It is so good to see you.'

She held out her hand and Sue grasped it warmly, almost knocked over by the warmth of the girl's welcome.

'We were sorry we couldn't meet you,' the girl was saying. 'I'm Jemima, by the way. We telephoned a message to the airport, but maybe it wasn't announced in time. But, here you are, anyway, so God is good. Would you like a drink? Cool water is in the vendor . . . or tea, if you would like some?'

'Water is fine.' Sue accepted gratefully, only then realising how thirsty she was. She must remember to always carry water with her.

'Pastor Jacob is busy in the school at the moment but he will see you as soon as he is free,' Jemima was saying. 'If you'd like to leave your suitcase here, I will show you around a little.'

Half-an-hour passed swiftly as Sue accompanied Jemima around the complex of buildings. Jemima explained how the orphanage had started a number of years ago, when a girl at their smaller centre in the city had contracted AIDS and had had to be passed on to a hospice with the right facilities to be able to help her.

'Pastor Jacob said that never again would he see such anguish in that little girl's face as she was taken away from the only home and family that she knew. It made him determined to open a centre where such children could be treated. He prayed for a building, and the first bungalow was given to him by a benefactor. Since then . . . '

Jemima paused and swung round her arm, indicating the assorted dwellings around them. 'Since then, one by one, we have purchased many of these other dwellings, using funds that God constantly sends our way and we care for seventy-eight children at the moment. We never have much money, but we have plenty of love to give away.'

Sue felt a lump in her throat as she listened. 'That's wonderful,' she said, strangely moved by Jemima's tale.

She blinked away a threatened tear and was glad she had done so for Jemima suddenly said, 'Ah, here's Pastor Jacob now. Come and meet him.'

Sue followed her to where a tall, dark-skinned man was striding down the track with a small boy seated on his shoulders. He looked to be in his middle forties, she guessed.

'Good day!' he boomed. 'You must be Amu's dear friend. Welcome to The Sheepfold.'

Holding on to the legs of the boy with one hand, he held out the other and enveloped Sue's smaller hand in it.

'Good day,' she replied, immediately

captivated by his beaming smile. 'It is kind of you to have me here.'

'Not at all! The pleasure is ours. I'm sure you'll find yourself helping in some way. Our children usually work their way into the hearts of our visitors.' Without waiting for a response, he gestured towards her companion. 'Has Jemima showed you where you will be staying?'

'Not yet. She has been telling me about how you started the orphanage and how it developed here. It's a moving story, Pastor Jacob.'

'God has been good,' he agreed, patting the legs dangling in front of his chest. 'He sends a bundle of love with every child who comes to our doors, just like with Yip, here.'

'And a bundle of mischief, no doubt!' Sue added, catching the glint in Yip's eyes.

'Mischief and boys go together, Miss Anders. Don't forget, I was once one myself!' Jacob lowered himself towards the ground and helped Yip to slide off his shoulders.

'Off you run, Yip. Find Mrs Bridget and tell her Amu's friend is here. My wife will come and take you to your room, Miss Anders . . . and then I will take you to Amu's aunt's home. Her aunt has been taken ill and Amu has had to stay with her to take care of her. She is a good girl and dutiful niece.'

While she waited for the pastor's wife to come, Sue collected her suitcase from the office and was waiting once more outside when a dark-skinned, homely-looking woman came towards her, eagerly towed along by a chattering Yip.

'Call me Bridget, dear . . . and may we call you Sue?'

Chattering pleasantly as they walked, pointing out different buildings such as the nursery and playroom for the under-fives, the sleeping quarters, schoolrooms and dining places for the older ones, Bridget led the way to one of the many cream-washed bungalows. It was sparsely furnished with furniture that had seen better days.

There was a small sitting-room containing two sagging sofas and a low table; and three rooms each with a single bed, an open cupboard with a clean but faded curtain hanging in front, a small table and a folding chair.

'We were pleased to be able to offer you a room,' Bridget told her. 'If you will just leave your case here for now, Jacob will take you to see Amu. I need to get on with organising the older girls with their cleaning duties. Maybe later or tomorrow you would like to accompany me and see some of our work here?'

Sue's heart gave a lurch as she imagined the children on their knees scrubbing the floors but she answered automatically, 'Yes, I'd love that. Thank you.'

During the ten-minute return drive through the suburbs, Jacob talked about different aspects of their work with the children and how grateful they were for the help of the volunteers who gave some of their time, taking her mind off the rigours of hardship the children themselves might have to submit to.

'A group called *The British Women In Malaysia* have taken us under their wing to some extent, and a few of them come one day a week to play and talk with the under-fives. If the children can learn to speak English,' he explained, 'they will have some chance of getting work when they are older, as Amu has done. Without that, since they haven't been registered at birth, and thus can't be registered to go to school . . . they wouldn't stand a chance in life.'

'I'll help whilst I'm here,' Sue immediately offered. After all, there was only so much sightseeing she could do on her own and she hated to be idle.

Amu's aunt's apartment was in an inner-city suburb about half-way between the orphanage and the tall Petronas Towers that marked the city centre, and Jacob slowed to a stop by a cluster of high-rise dwellings, with cream rendered walls. There were no pavings around the buildings and the track was pitted with holes but the area was clean and the ground around each dwelling was surprisingly green.

Jacob told Sue the number of Aunt Rathi's apartment and then excused himself, as he had other calls to make. 'Will you be able to make your own way back to The Sheepfold?' he asked.

Sue assured him that that was no problem and entered the dim building. Not caring to trust the lift, she went up three flights of stairs and rang the bell on number 354, waiting a little anxiously for the door to be opened.

When it did, a pretty dark-skinned young woman of Sue's age stood beaming on the threshold. 'Sue! You are here!' Then she paused, suddenly looking shyly at Sue, suddenly unsure of herself.

'Amu!' Sue responded, holding out her arms, and the two girls embraced, clinging tightly to each other, unable to speak.

Eventually, Sue drew back a little, her hands still clasping Amu's arms, not wanting to let go of the simply dressed, dark-haired Malaysian girl. She felt an emotional lump in her throat and an instant bond of belonging. With her recent conversation with the pastor about the orphans fresh in her mind, it occurred to Sue that Amu was the 'sister' she had never had, and she had an uncanny sense of knowing that, somehow, their destinies were entwined.

2

David Blake settled in the silver-grey limousine, thankful for the air-conditioning. He had only been away for a week but the heat had hit him as he stepped outside the airport building. No wonder that attractive English girl had been taken aback by it!

He twisted his head around and gazed over his shoulder to where he could see the girl stooping to slip into the taxi pulled from the rank. Maybe he should have offered her a lift?

He instantly shook his head. As the junior partner in a small accountancy firm, he had enough to think about, without adding any other complications to his life.

A frown creased his tanned face as he reflected on the conference he had attended in Manchester where he had learned that a high-powered accountancy firm had put in an offer to merge with them.

Why hadn't Toby Naughton, his senior partner, thought fit to share this important information with him? Didn't he trust him? Surely his two years of being the junior partner had proved his worth and his loyalty to the firm.

It was a wonder that the unexpected snippet of information hadn't caused an embarrassing incident. Although inwardly flummoxed by the information, he knew that, beyond the merest twitch of a muscle in his cheek, he hadn't betrayed his ignorance of the matter. He could thank his upbringing for that.

In a house full of teenage boys, the only private place he had had was within his mind. No-one could sneak in there and remove its contents . . . as had constantly happened to any personal belongings not under lock and key.

'It's good to have you back, David,' the attractive woman at his side murmured softly. She had followed his twisted glance over his shoulder but hadn't seen anything or anyone of interest. 'Anything new at the conference?'

'You could say so, Asleena,' David replied tightly. 'Is Toby at the office today?'

Asleena Mawan, his partner's personal assistant, shook her head. Her sleek dark hair was swept up into a French pleat, accentuating her cheekbones. Her red lips pouted slightly.

'Unfortunately, there has been a slight delay in his return from holiday. He was involved in a car accident a week last Friday night and he has been detained in hospital.'

David stared at her incredulously. 'So, he's still in Australia, is he? And didn't anyone think to let me know? I wouldn't have gone to the conference if I'd known. Or, at the very least, I would have returned a day or so sooner. How badly hurt is he?'

Asleena laid her red manicured fingernails on his arm and smiled conciliatorily at him. 'Toby said not to worry you, David. He isn't badly injured and didn't want news of the accident to become common knowledge at the conference, which would have inevitably happened if you had had to leave suddenly.'

'He obviously doesn't give me much credit for discretion, does he?' David said with a note of bitterness in his voice. 'When is he due back?'

'Any day, he hopes. He was as annoyed about it as you are, but his medical insurers insist he stays there until discharged by the medical staff or else his insurance will be made null and void.'

David made an impatient gesture, inadvertently shaking his arm free of Asleena's light touch, and stared morosely out of the window, wondering how much Asleena knew of the merger plans. Probably more than he did.

Usually a loyal and discreet man, he moodily began to reflect that he knew very little about his partner's life outside the office. All David knew was that he was married but with no children; that he lived in a much grander apartment than he did and that he belonged to a number of exclusive clubs that gave him access to the leaders of Malaysian commerce and banking.

Naturally, Toby creamed off the more affluent clients who came their way, at the same time assuring David that when he had proved himself capable of handling the affairs of the run-of-the-mill accounts, he would have earned the right to manage the affairs of the wealthy. That carrot had dangled before his nose for two years and he was eager to take a bite.

'I'll give Toby a ring,' he said decisively to Asleena as their limousine drew up in front of the tower block that housed their office.

Their driver leaped out of the driving seat to hold open Asleena's door. She slipped elegantly from the seat and joined David on the pavement. 'That won't be possible, I'm afraid,' she informed him lightly. 'His mobile is switched off and he hasn't said which hospital he's in.'

David stared at her in disbelief. 'That's ridiculous! How does he expect us to run the business with him out of contact? We're working to a tight enough schedule as it is! We need more help in the office. I've a good mind to hire a 'temp' while he's away.'

Completely annoyed, he strode ahead of her towards the lifts and jabbed the button.

Asleena's high-heeled shoes clattered behind him on the marble floor. 'You know he won't like that,' she argued. 'We're not in a position to take on more staff. He wants to wait until . . . '

Her voice tailed off.

' . . . until what?' David questioned, his right eyebrow raised questioningly. So, she did know about the proposed merger.

'Er . . . until this year's accounts are settled,' Asleena said quickly, as they stepped into the lift.

Since the lift was already occupied, David felt unable to comment further until they were inside their own premises. Normally an even-tempered man, the delay gave him time to calm his ruffled temper and he was able to return the greeting of his own secretary, Ko Siew Mei, without any sign of irritation.

Ko Siew Mei, a Chinese Malaysian girl, scuttled back behind her desk and began to type industriously as David and Asleena went into Toby's office.

'Now, David, there's no need to get into a huff about anything,' Asleena protested before he could speak. 'You know very well that Toby thinks very highly of you. He doesn't want any of our clients to know about his accident in case they start to panic about their affairs not receiving the attention they merit, especially right now whilst we are doing the end-of-year tax returns.'

'Now, that puzzles me, Asleena,' David said slowly, watching her face for any sign of anxiety. 'Just what is going on to make us wary of what our competitors think?'

'Why, nothing, David dear. Whatever makes you think . . . ?'

'Because I'm not stupid, Asleena. When I hear news of an impending merger from one of our competitors at the conference, a subject never broached in my presence, I begin to wonder just what is going on and why I, the junior partner, know nothing about it, whereas you so obviously do.'

For a moment Asleena seemed taken aback but swiftly recovered her poise and reached out towards David in a gesture of helplessness. 'Toby had every intention of mentioning it to you on his return from holiday.'

'Mentioning? Just what does that mean? This is something that will totally alter the structure of our partnership.'

'Yes, well, he's aware of that. That was why he wanted to be sure about which way to go before telling you about it!'

'And I get no say in the matter? Listen, Asleena, I don't care how you do it, but I want you to get hold of Toby some time today and tell him that I insist on talking to him. And if that doesn't happen, I shall seriously reconsider my position here.'

'I'm not sure I . . . '

'Just do it, Asleena. You know where to find me.'

He stalked out of Toby's office and into his own, casting little more than a glance at the feverishly typing Ko.

In exasperation, he pulled open his filing cabinet and took out a sheaf of files he had been working on before his short absence, and switched on his computer. The end-of-year reckoning for tax returns was looming closer than was comfortable, especially with Toby's absence. He had better get his own clients' affairs settled in case he needed to do any work on Toby's.

It was about an hour later when Ko knocked gently on the door and, on hearing his response, stepped into the inner office, her honey-coloured cheeks burning red.

'Excuse me, Mr Blake, sir. There's a gentlemen here, Raju Razak, wanting . . . demanding . . . an appointment with Mr Naughton and won't listen when I say he isn't available. Will you be able to see him, do you think? I know Mr Naughton likes to keep his clients separate from yours but . . . ' She anxiously flickered her eyes over her shoulder to where the irate client was waiting.

David frowned at the reminder that there was a two-tier hierarchy in the partnership. 'Can't Asleena deal with him, Ko? She will be familiar with his account.'

'But, Mr Blake, Asleena isn't here. She left the office over half an hour ago and didn't say when she will be back. What shall I tell him? He is very angry,' she added in a whisper. 'He says he will take his business elsewhere if his account isn't sorted today.'

David sighed and clicked off the file

that was open on his computer. 'OK, that's fine, Ko,' he said, smiling reassuringly at her. 'I've got no appointments of my own today. Send him in and see if you can get at his file. I'll try to stall him.'

Ko ushered in a small, slender man. His face unsmiling, he barely touched David's outstretched hand and refused to sit down.

'This will not do, Mr Blake. I am accustomed to dealing with the senior partner. Mr Naughton deals with my account and I do not like to be relegated to his assistant! Mr Naughton assured me that he would have everything sorted by the end of last week but, this morning, I received a demand from the tax office for my up-to-date accounts, with the threat of a fine if they are not submitted in time!'

David forced a smile on to his face. 'Please be seated, Mr Razak,' he said calmly, indicating the chair again. 'Mr Naughton isn't here today, but I am perfectly well qualified to look into your account. My secretary is getting your file from my partner's office. Shall we take a look at it together?'

'Hmph! I suppose so,' Mr Razak ungraciously assented.

David waited until the man was seated before seating himself at the other side of the desk, feeling the frustration of being the under-valued junior partner.

'Ah, here she is. Thank you, Ko.' He smiled briefly at her and took the proffered file out of her hand. Quickly, he scanned the cover for the date of its previous review, relieved to note that it was only ten days ago.

'You'll be glad to know that Mr Naughton was working on your file just before he went on holiday, Mr Razak. Unfortunately, his return has been delayed slightly. Nothing to worry about,' he added quickly. 'We are expecting him any day, as soon as . . . er . . . as soon as he can get a flight,' he temporised, hoping it would be so.

'Is my account ready or not?' Mr

Razak demanded, his voice taut with anxiety. 'That is all I am anxious to know. It must be submitted by the end of this week!'

David glanced inside the file and could immediately see that the paperwork had not been brought up to date. He surmised that it must be still in progress on Toby's computer, and Toby's *special clients* were held on limited access by password only. Drat Asleena. Why did she choose today to take extra time off?

'I will inform Mr Naughton's secretary about the problem the moment she comes in, Mr Razak, and will see that your account is completed by tomorrow afternoon,' David promised, forcing a smile.

Mr Razak didn't return the smile. 'This is very awkward, Mr Blake. What am I to do? I placed my business with your firm in good faith on the highest recommendation. I don't pay a top rate of fee for second-class service!'

David fought to keep his expression

neutral. 'I will give your account my immediate attention, Mr Razak and, no doubt Mr Naughton will discount your fee accordingly. Now, is there anything else I can do for you?'

He knew perfectly well that there wasn't, but he was finding it difficult to restrain himself. If Toby had walked through the door at that moment, he would have handed in his notice with no more ado!

The disgruntled client tersely declined any further help. 'I will give you until tomorrow afternoon!' he repeated. 'And if I am not satisfied, my business goes elsewhere! Is that clear?'

David half-rose to see the man to the door but his action was needless. With a curt nod, Mr Razak strode out of the office and was gone.

David leaned back in his chair and sighed in exasperation. He had kept saying to Toby that he should have access to all the files and today proved him right.

Determined to do something positive

to bring the dispute between him and Toby into the open, he reached forward and picked up the telephone. If he had to ring every hospital in Brisbane, he would do so.

3

Sue smiled fondly at Amu. It was hard to believe that they had only just met. 'You are just how you seemed in your letters, Amu ... and you'll look absolutely gorgeous in this dress,' she assured the Malaysian girl, admiring the colourful silk creation that Amu was holding in front of her. 'I'm looking forward to meeting your fiancé.'

'He is working away at the moment. I think I told you in a letter.' A tiny frown clouded Amu's bright face. 'My aunt plans that we will live here with her when we are married, as Vishnu works away quite often, and it is my duty to repay her for taking care of me. But I think I would prefer to start on our own.'

'I should think so!' Sue agreed. 'I'm sure Vishnu will agree with you.'

'My aunt has a very strong mind,'

Amu said softly. 'She generally gets her own way.'

'Mmm,' Sue agreed, thinking of her meeting with the bedridden Aunt Rathi half an hour earlier, and how often the older woman had stressed how grateful Amu needed to be for having been taken away from the orphanage.

'A dreadful place!' Aunt Rathi had declared, her voice strengthening in her vehemence. 'A filthy, down-trodden, flea-infested place!'

Amu's 'Oh, no, Aunt!' had been silenced by a fit of coughing from her aunt and, once Amu had settled her aunt down again, the two young woman had tiptoed out of the oppressive room. They were now conversing quietly in Amu's small bedroom, an alcove off the sitting-room.

Sue was surprised by the modern amenities in the house, having held in her mind a picture of a traditional Malaysian wooden house on stilts, although she realised that Amu had actually said very little in her letters about her aunt's home. Was that because she was unhappy here?

'At least you get out to go to work, Amu,' she consoled her friend. 'You have often told me how much you enjoy that. Will you still be able to do that when you are married?'

'Oh, yes, I must continue to work. My wage is important. That is why Aunt Rathi wants us to live here. As soon as she is better I must go back to my job before Mr Blake has to get someone else. I just hope he will understand that I cannot work this week. Oh!'

Suddenly, Amu was agitated and upset. Her hand flew to her mouth, her dark eyes filled with anxiety. 'He will be back from his business trip. I must let him know at once. Oh, dear! Will you sit with Aunt Rathi while I go to the telephone, Sue? I must telephone to his office immediately.'

Sue glanced through the window, amazed to see that it was raining. 'But you will get wet, Amu! It's pouring down!'

'It rains each afternoon. It is nothing. I must go!' She grabbed hold of an umbrella from by the door and hurried outside.

Whilst Amu was out, Sue went twice in response to Aunt Rathi's demand for her pillows to be plumped up and for a drink of cool water.

'Where has that ungrateful girl gone?' she demanded. 'She knows I need her by my side.'

'Amu's gone to telephone her boss,' Sue explained, 'to apologise for being unable to get to work this week. She won't be long.'

'Huh! That's what you know! She will waste her time chattering to anyone she meets. She's a lazy girl.'

'Oh, I'm sure she's not.' Sue defended her friend. 'The pastor at the orphanage said what a good worker she is. You should be proud of her.'

'I'd be more proud of her if she did what I tell her and got a job at the hospital. She would get longer hours there and bring home much more money. But, no, she is a selfish girl and won't do anything I tell her. No gratitude, that's what it is! No gratitude!'

Sue found it upsetting to hear Amu spoken of in such a way and she was relieved when her friend returned home. Amu was soaking wet and her glum face told her that her mission hadn't succeeded.

'What's the matter, Amu? Won't he let you have time off? I thought you said he is a good employer.'

Amu shook her head. 'It's not that. I couldn't get through and people were waiting to use the telephone. I'll have to try again later, maybe when he gets home. I do not want to let him down.'

Sue had an idea. 'You work as his maid, don't you? What do you do?'

Amu spread out her hands. 'I clean his apartment, wash his clothes and iron them, do any shopping that he needs. Sometimes I cook him a simple meal but generally he eats out. I rarely see him, really, as he works until quite late at night. He leaves me a note if he wants anything different to be done. As I said, he is a good employer. I don't want to lose my job with him.'

'Why don't I do your job for you, Amu? It will only be for a few days, I'm sure. You've told me he lives right in the city centre so I'll be able to find his place. I'll write him a note to tell him of our arrangement.'

'But you are here on holiday, Sue! You must not take up your time working.'

'I'm not used to being a lady of leisure.' Sue laughed. 'There'll be plenty of time to do some sightseeing. And, anyway, I'll be pleased to help you out. Pastor Jacob said how difficult it is to find jobs in the city. This way, you won't be in danger of losing yours.'

Much relieved, Amu agreed and she told Sue how to find Mr Blake's apartment block and gave her the key to his apartment. 'If you get there for nine o'clock in the morning, he will have gone to work and you probably

41

won't even see him,' Amu assured her. 'But, in any case, he is a very nice man and I'm sure he will understand.'

With the arrangement settled, Amu walked with Sue to the end of the road. Thankfully, the rain had stopped.

'I'll come and see you when I have finished work tomorrow,' Sue promised Amu, as a taxi she had hailed drew into the kerb at her side.

★　★　★

David was surprised when Asleena returned to the office in mid-afternoon. He gave her a few minutes to settle in and then followed her into Toby's office. Asleena was seated behind Toby's desk, filing her nails. She paused the action and glanced up at him. 'Yes?'

'So good of you to return, Asleena,' he said, his voice heavy with sarcasm, wondering why she always brought out the worst in him. Probably because he suspected that she was closer to Toby than she ought to be to a married man.

Asleena pouted. 'Toby doesn't mind me going to have my hair done when he's not here. You know I'll make up the time if need be.'

'That's not the point. One of Toby's clients came to see him and you weren't here.'

'Oh? Which one?'

'Raju Razak. He is anxious to have his accounts settled and tax returns completed by tomorrow afternoon and was justifiably annoyed that I was unable to help him. Look, Asleena, there's no sign of Toby getting back here before then. You'd better let me see the work that Toby has done so far and I'll burn the midnight oil to get it finished for him.'

Asleena looked startled. 'You know that Toby's clients prefer to have their accounts seen to solely by him, David. They won't be happy if they get to know the junior partner has worked on them.'

'They needn't necessarily know,' David replied reasonably. 'We are nearing the year-end and these accounts need to be finalised. Razak was angry and threatens to move his business elsewhere if they aren't ready by tomorrow. There are other files pending as well.'

'Yes, but . . . '

'There are no 'buts', Asleena. Either find a way to get in touch with Toby, or give me the password to his files. I've spent over an hour this morning trying to find out which hospital he's in, without any success. For heaven's sake, Asleena, what is it with the man? He can't run an accountancy firm and be incommunicado for over a week.'

'It's hardly Toby's fault that he is stuck in hospital in northern Europe,' Asleena protested.

David felt thunderstruck. 'Northern Europe? He said he was holidaying in Australia.'

Asleena tightened her lips. 'He changed his mind. Anyway, it's immaterial where he is. The fact is he has to stay there until he gets discharged. It's just as much a pain to him as it is to you.'

'Maybe! But, it's me that's facing the

clients. And I'm determined not to let this business go under just because Toby has some strange idea of not letting me know where he is. I want the password, Asleena. In Toby's absence, I'm the one in charge.'

Asleena hesitated only slightly in the face of David's uncharacteristic outburst. With her lips pursed tightly, she inserted a key into a small drawer and pulled it open. Taking out a small notebook, she copied down a string of numbers.

'He changes these numbers every week, so they are only of use until Friday. Then, they will automatically change. This is on your own head, David. I shall make it clear to Toby that I have given them to you under duress.'

'And I will make it clear to Toby that something has to change here if we are to continue to work harmoniously together.'

He took the piece of paper out of her hand then strode back to his own office and immediately brought up Toby's screen on to his computer. He swiftly identified which accounts needed to be worked on before the end of the month and copied them on to his own screen. The work would keep him busy for the rest of the week, overtime included, but that was what he relished. Figures and mathematical formulae, the bread and butter of his work, were like manna from heaven.

It wasn't long before he had identified a number of inconsistencies in Razak's file, but however much he tried to back-track, he couldn't get to the root of it.

Asleena disclaimed all knowledge. 'Leave it to Toby,' she advised. 'I'm sure he'll be home in a day or so.'

'A day or so will be too late for Mr Razak,' David reminded her.

It was close on midnight when he gave up for the day. He rotated his shoulders backwards and stretched his arms above his head, easing the dull ache. Hating to be defeated by a column of figures, he nonetheless knew he needed some sleep and carefully backed up his work before switching off the computer.

It was after nine o'clock in the morning before Sue awoke and her brain didn't really want to waken then, but once Sue had seen the time she leaped out of bed and rushed into the small bathroom.

To her brain and body, it was still only one o'clock in the morning. Ah, well, hopefully, people would understand. Once dressed, she made her way outside, where, again the humid temperature unexpectedly hit her. Eventually she found Bridget busily organising some teenage girls with their morning chores.

Morning chores were an integral part of orphanage life, Sue reflected ruefully. She supposed someone had to do the cleaning and, in this situation, who else but the youngsters themselves?

Sue had told Bridget of her change of plans when she had returned the previous day and now, after telling the girls to start their work, Bridget showed Sue where to find bread, butter, milk and coffee for breakfast.

'Help yourself, dear. We don't stand on ceremony here. Will you be back for lunch, do you think?'

'No. If it's all right with you, I'll have lunch out and then go to see Amu again. Now, I've got Mr Blake's address so I'll be off as soon as I've eaten.'

'Did you manage to get in touch with him, dear?'

Sue shook her head. 'No, but, hopefully, I'll have been and gone before he gets home. I'll write a note to explain what's happened.'

It was half-past ten when Sue arrived at the tall building that housed David Blake's apartment. It wasn't far from the city centre where the impressive Petronas Twin Towers stood over an ultra-modern shopping mall, where Amu had advised Sue to go for her lunch later.

As she paid the taxi fare and stepped aside, a male voice hailed the taxi, its owner almost colliding with her in his haste to engage the taxi before it drew away from the kerbside.

As he leaped inside, Sue noticed that his briefcase was open and shouted, 'Hey!'

The man half-turned, knocking his briefcase against the side of the door.

Sue was astonished to recognise him as the man who had spoken to her at the airport the day before but, as her heart leaped within causing her breath to catch in surprise, the man turned away and dived into the rear seat of the taxi. Without delay, the taxi slid into the stream of passing traffic and was instantly swallowed out of sight.

Sue berated herself for her gauche response to her recognition of the man. So, he was a good-looking man. So what? She smiled ruefully, acknowledging that she obviously hadn't made a similar impact on him at their earlier brief encounter!

As she turned away, she noticed a small packet on the edge of the kerb.

She bent to pick it up, instantly recognising it as a pack of back-up discs out of a computer. She stared around. Where had the man come from? There were a number of apartment blocks nearby. He could have come from any one of them.

What did one do here in Malaysia? Did they have police stations, as in Britain where one could take lost property? She had better ask Amu or Pastor Jacob. She slipped the packet into her bag and, after a moment's scrutiny, identified the apartment block of Amu's employer.

Not feeling confident enough to ask the security guards what to do with the packet, she merely showed them Amu's security card and walked up the steep driveway. The ground floor was spacious and impressive with a creamy-peach marble floor and walls. Amu's key and security card got Sue past the security system and she made her way by lift up to the fifth floor and apartment 3A.

She was pleasantly surprised by its size and modern décor, although its minimalist style wasn't her particular favourite. For a bachelor-pad it was ideal, and from a cleaner's point of view, she reflected with some relief. Apparently, Mr Blake had been away for a week and so there was no washing or ironing to be done. Just a freshening up of the apartment and clearing away of any breakfast remains.

She had just finished the final task of tidying up the bedroom, when she heard a noise from the main lounge. It sounded as if someone had entered the apartment. Slightly apprehensive, she went to the doorway and stepped into the lounge.

She stopped in amazement. The *intruder*, a man dressed in a dark lounge-suit, was no other than the man she already met twice before — at the airport and just after she had got out of the taxi earlier in the day. He, too, halted abruptly, his face betraying shock at her presence.

'Who on earth are you?' he demanded harshly.

'I . . . I'm Amu's friend,' Sue stammered, aware that the man had no previous knowledge of her. She hadn't managed to get through to him on the telephone and neither had she written the promised note of explanation. She had meant to do it before she left.

'I got in with Amu's key. I've come to clean your apartment.'

'Amu? My maid? It's her job to clean my apartment! Why isn't she here? Why has she sent you?'

He seemed very angry, and Sue was beginning to regret her impulsive offer. She should have made more effort to contact him but, with his probable presence in the apartment having been discounted, she had thought it unnecessary. Now, she wished she had acted otherwise.

'Amu's aunt is ill,' she stammered. 'She doesn't know how long she will be unable to come and was afraid you might get someone else in her place. I offered to come instead.' She spread her hands around. 'Er . . . I've just about finished. I was about to leave,' she finished lamely.

David Blake snapped his lips together. 'Then, I think you'd better go,' he agreed shortly. 'No, hang on! I'll check the rooms to make sure . . . '

Sue felt a flash of indignation well up within her. How dare he! 'You will find nothing missing!' she hotly declared. 'I came to do you a favour, to save you any inconvenience Amu's absence might have caused. I can see that I may as well have saved myself the trouble!'

He turned back to face her, reluctant admiration hovering in his slightly sardonic glance. His right eyebrow rose perceptively and, for a moment, quite outside her own control, Sue felt her insides begin to melt as a shaft of fire spiralled through her.

'When you've checked all the family silver, I will take my leave of you,' she said with a trace of her own sarcasm. 'I apologise on Amu's behalf and hope you won't hold it against her. It was an on-the-spur-of-the-moment decision to help out, obviously the wrong one. I am totally to blame. I'm sorry. Goodbye!'

When he didn't reply, Sue snatched up her shoulder bag and walked as calmly as she could towards the door. As she walked past him, he put a hand on her arm.

'Not so fast, young lady!'

She turned to face him, almost gasping as his touch sent an electric shiver coursing up her arm.

'I want to know your name and where you are staying, in case of further enquiries, and I demand the return of Amu's key and security card, if you don't mind!'

The last four words were spoken heavy with sarcasm and sent a sigh of hopeless whirling through Sue's head. He must mean to terminate Amu's employment, after all!

'Oh, don't . . . '

He snapped out his hand. 'Key . . . and name!'

Sue wryly pressed her lips together and, her hands shaking in her distress at Amu's misfortune, began to rummage inside her bag for the key and card.

'My name is Sue Anders. I've been Amu's friend for years, although we only met yesterday. I'm staying . . .'

Her bag slipped from her hand and spilled out on to the floor. She dropped down to the floor to hastily scoop her belongings back into her bag . . . lip salve, comb, small purse, ah, Amu's key and security card . . . and the back-up discs she had picked up outside on the pavement.

Unaccountably, it was the pack of discs that she picked up first . . . but, as her fingers curled around it, a grip of iron clasped her hand.

Thoroughly startled she looked up to see David Blake crouched down in front of her, his steely grey eyes level with her own. Any trace of warmth that might have lingered since his entry into the apartment was now gone . . . replaced by cold anger and contempt, Sue recognised in bewilderment.

'What?'

'Nothing taken, huh?'

He prised open her fingers and took the back-up discs from her hand, straightening up his body and drawing her to her feet also.

'What's your game, young lady?' he asked softly. 'And who sent you here?'

4

'Game?' Sue faltered, realising by David Blake's forbidding expression that this was something more than a mild accusation of pilfering.

'Precisely! Who is behind you? What are you up to?' David's voice snapped into her whirling brain.

Sue shook her head, as much to attempt to clear it as in denial of his words. 'I don't know what you mean. I picked them up outside on the pavement. You know, just after you nearly knocked me over diving into the taxi I had just vacated. I was going to ask Amu where I should take it. Are they yours?'

David looked startled by her words. His eyes narrowed as he gazed at her face. The force of his anger drained away from his face and he seemed an altogether different person.

'So, it was you! I did wonder.'

His eyes narrowed again and a look of suspicion crept back into his expression. 'I saw you at the airport yesterday, as well. You've been following me, haven't you? Were you on my plane? Have you followed me from England?'

His grip on her hand tightened, though Sue hardly noticed it. She felt a tiny surge of triumph zip around her body. He had noticed her! Even so, the conceit of the man!

'Huh! Don't flatter yourself!' she retorted, ineffectively attempting to tug free her hand. 'Why on earth should I follow you? I don't even know you! I hadn't even heard of you until Amu was so fearful of losing her job.'

Still unnerved by his accusations, she decided that attack was better than defence.

'You wouldn't get away with it in England, you know! Sacking someone just because they had to look after a sick relative. It's called harassment, though I don't suppose you employers are under the same threat of being prosecuted here in Malaysia, but that's no excuse for you to make life difficult for Amu. And do you mind letting go of my hand. You're hurting me!'

David looked taken aback by the ferocity of her verbal attack and she could see indecision creeping into his eyes. Also, she noticed a glimmer of incredulously, she wondered if it were admiration, except she found that difficult to believe. Amu wouldn't be in fear of losing her job if David Blake had an ounce of compassion in his body. Even so, she relaxed a little and, realising she might have put Amu's job more in jeopardy by her belligerent attitude towards him, she forced a laugh.

'It really is a coincidence that we had met before, and I truly didn't know who you were. And . . . ' She winced. 'You really are hurting my hand!'

David stared at her, detecting the ring of truth in her voice. He glanced down at his hand and was surprised to see that he was gripping hers so tightly it was changing colour. For some reason, his throat felt tight and he felt all the fight draining out of him.

'I . . . I'm sorry,' he apologised. 'Only there's been some strange things happening and it seemed . . . '

He mentally shook his head to clear it. When he had arrived at the office and discovered that all of his work on Raju Razak's account had somehow been deleted from his computer overnight, he had been stopped in his tracks. He was sure he had backed everything up properly the previous evening, late though it was.

And he was just as sure that he had put the back-up disc into his briefcase. When he had then discovered that the discs were missing, he had known a moment of panic. Razak was due back before the end of the afternoon and he had nothing to show him.

And the girl's account of finding the discs on the pavement rang true. He knew he had put them in his briefcase, and he had found the clasp to be open when he arrived at the office.

All the same, something strange was happening, but for the life of him he couldn't think why. Why was Toby keeping out of his way? Was he in some spot of bother? He couldn't imagine it. Toby Naughton was a successful businessman, full of bonhomie. So what if his lifestyle was slightly over-extravagant?

Even he, a junior partner had a plush enough apartment and a maid to do all his housekeeping, which brought him back to the matter in hand.

Did he believe what this girl had to say? She seemed genuine, and there was something about her that sent all kinds of strange and not unpleasant sensa-tions chasing helter-skelter through his body.

He relaxed his grip on her hand and felt cut adrift when she pulled it away from him. Her long hair fell neatly around her face and, even as he thought about it . . . wanted, even, to reach out and touch it . . . she raised her right hand and tucked some strands behind her ears as if she were putting it out of his reach.

The small action seemed like a challenge to his male ego. He was unused to the uncertainty he was experiencing. He was the one who did the challenging, the choosing, the chase, the conquest. The one who sets the limits . . . no commitment; no shackles.

He suddenly realised that he didn't want her to walk out of his door and, if by some mischance, she was a part of whatever was happening, then he wanted her to be where he could keep an eye on her and he might discover what was behind it all.

He raised his right eyebrow as, once more, he held out his hand. 'The security pass and key, Miss . . . Anders, was it?'

He saw her flinch slightly. Was that because she had failed in her mission?

It was only when she stooped down that he realised that they were still on the floor at her feet alongside her shoulder bag. She picked up her bag with her left hand and scooped up the key and card with her right and placed the two items into his outstretched hand.

'Please don't blame Amu, Mr Blake. Her aunt is a bit of a tyrant and Amu is desperate not to lose her job. Her aunt wants her to become a cleaner at the hospital but Amu is happier working for you. I know she is.'

A twist of her expression seemed to indicate that the thought of that was preposterous, recalling her earlier censure of his character, David found it difficult to suppress a wry grin. He wasn't used to being regarded as an ogre or a bad employer.

However, much as he wished he had the time to question her further, time was passing and the pressure of work to be done was irresistible. 'I need to get back to my office, Miss Anders. I think perhaps you had better tell me where you are staying and I will get in touch with you later. If I am then satisfied that this was nothing more than a misjudged effort to help your friend, I will say no more about it. Amu is a capable girl and I have no wish to replace her with someone I don't know.'

A relieved smile flooded Sue's face. 'Thank you,' she said sincerely. 'I'll be happy to comply with that. I'm staying at the orphanage called The Sheepfold. I'm sure Pastor Jacob will vouch for me. He has only known me since yesterday but he knows Amu very well and he knew of my intention of coming here today, and I did keep trying to telephone you, both at your office and here, but the former was continually engaged and there was no answer from here.'

David nodded. That figured. He'd been using his phone extensively trying to trace Toby and, although he had been at the office until after midnight, all calls were automatically transferred here once office hours were over.

'I know Pastor Jacob well. I'll be in touch.' He paused, glancing around the room. 'You seem to have done a good job here, anyway,' he added. 'If Jacob verifies your tale, you may continue until Amu is able to return.'

Sue wished she could tell him what to do with his job, but knew that that wouldn't be fair to Amu.

Besides, he really was quite dishy when he relaxed, and she had to force herself to act as if he meant nothing more than a prospective temporary employer, when, really, her thoughts were running on entirely different lines altogether!

The rest of the day seemed rather an anti-climax after its eventful start. Sue strolled around the KLCC, the modern shopping mall at the base of the Petronas Twin Towers and had lunch in Strudels, an internationally renowned street café. She then took a taxi to Amu's aunt's home and tried to reassure Amu that her job was safe.

'I hope so.' Amu sighed. 'No other

boss would pay me to work part-time at the orphanage, like he does.'

Sue gasped in surprise. 'Does he?'

'Yes. He says as long as I keep his place tidy and do the necessary tasks for him, I can help Pastor and Mother Bridget in the rest of my time. He even pays for my taxi fares back and forth. Like I told you, he is nice, kind man.'

'Mmm, so it would seem,' Sue murmured, uncomfortably remembering some of the accusations she had hurled at the man. It seemed she might have to revise some of her thoughts of him. Still, it didn't mean he was a saint, did it. He was only doing his best to hang on to a good maid and, no doubt, salving his conscience at the same time.

Their conversation was constantly interrupted by Aunt Rathi irritably calling Amu to her side every ten minutes or so and, eventually, Sue decided it would be for the best if she left Amu in peace to see to her aunt's needs.

'It's a sign she's getting better,' she

said unconvincingly, slipping her feet back into her shoes as they parted company on the doorstep. 'I'll come and see you again tomorrow. Is there anything I can bring you?'

Having been assured that a neighbour did any necessary shopping, Sue returned to the orphanage to see if there was something she could do there as a way of repaying the pastor and his wife for their hospitality and also to update them on the morning's events, to forewarn them of David Blake's intention to check up on her.

'That will be no problem,' Bridget assured her, as they scrubbed vegetables together for the children's evening meal. 'David is a very kind man. He is one of our patrons and does his best to find employment for our young people when they are old enough to start work. He must be under much pressure at work if he is as irritable as you describe him.'

'Well, I suppose I did rather catch him on the hop,' Sue excused her criticism of him.

'On the hop?' Bridget repeated, her forehead creased in a frown.

'Unexpectedly,' Sue said as an alternative.

'Ah, I understand. You see, Sue, this is why it is good for English people to come and talk with our children. Jacob and I can both speak English quite well but we don't know your colloquial expressions. Why don't you go along to one of the common rooms now that lessons are over for the day? Did you bring any western magazines with you? The girls would love to see western fashion, and the boys, too!'

Yes, she had brought two magazines to read on the flight. Taking up the suggestion, Sue eventually found a bungalow with half a dozen teenage girls in it, scrapping noisily over an ancient magazine that was almost in tatters.

After their initial shyness was overcome, they eagerly settled down to thumbing their way through the pages of the two new magazines, asking Sue question after question about life in the western world. Their lack of personal possessions reminded Sue of all that she now took for granted, even though she too had a poor start in life. She remembered the days when nothing was her own, and anything she treasured was in danger of being taken by one or other of her many *sisters*.

Later, she asked Bridget how many teenage girls there were and asked if it would be all right for her to buy some hair accessories the following day. During her earlier saunter around the shopping mall she had noticed that such things were priced much more cheaply than in Britain and on receiving Bridget's approval, Sue made a mental note to purchase a selection of such items the following day.

5

Late that afternoon, David Blake faced the irate man seated on the other side of his desk and took a deep breath before he replied.

'Mr Razak, I have studied your accounts and, in my opinion, there are some items missing. There have to be, because the figures in this file don't correspond with those in this computer file. Is there anything you have told Mr Naughton that you haven't told me?'

Mr Razak stood up abruptly and leaned over the desk, his face red with anger. 'Are you accusing me of lying, Mr Blake?' he asked in outraged tones. 'I have repeatedly told you that Mr Naughton has all the relevant facts and he has assured me that everything is under control. I am not prepared to have the junior partner imply that I have been less than honest in my dealings! Where is your proof, I ask you? Where is it?'

David tried to appear calmer than he felt. 'I am not accusing you of anything, Mr Razak. All I am saying is that this file cannot contain the full accounts, because the two just don't rationalise. Something is missing and, until I know what it is, I cannot submit the file to the tax office. I won't put the reputation of this firm on the line like that.'

Mr Razak thumped the desk with his clenched fist. 'Mr Naughton knows all the necessary details. He said it would go through!'

'You must have misunderstood what he said. I'm saying it can't go through!'

'Then we have impasse, Mr Blake.''

David ruefully acknowledged the truth of that. However, he was reluctant to have to tell Toby on his return that they had lost the account.

'I will send the basic information and register your returns. That way, we can stall for time until Mr Naughton returns. I must also point out that you would be fortunate to get taken on by anyone else in the next few weeks. Everyone is working flat out with their current accounts.

Mr Razak drew himself up tall, looking anything but satisfied by his assurance. 'I would prefer it to be receiving Mr Naughton's fullest attention!' he said cuttingly. 'As you say, my hands are tied . . . for the time being. Have no doubt, I will be putting it in the hands of my solicitor if I am prosecuted because of your negligence. Good day!'

As he slammed his way out of the office, David leaned back in his chair. He leaned forward to buzz Ko but was forestalled by Asleena sweeping unannounced into the office. 'Toby is on the other phone,' she announced shortly. 'I've told him to hold the line.'

'Why didn't you transfer it into here?' David questioned as he rose to his feet. 'You know how anxious I have been to speak to him.'

'But you know it's not office policy to

interrupt an interview with a client, David,' Asleena smiled patronisingly.

'There can always be exceptions!' David snapped.

Fuming inwardly, he strode into Toby's office and snatched up the phone. The regular buzzing tone informed him immediately that Toby was no longer on line. Damn! He slammed the receiver back into its holder and turned on his heel, almost knocking Asleena over.

'He's gone!' he snapped.

'Oh, dear! Never mind. He told me to tell you that he wants you to put his clients' files aside until he returns. I did warn you!'

David ignored the snub. 'Did he say when he's coming back?'

'Hopefully, the doctor will discharge him later on today. He's just as desperate for his discharge as you are!'

'Did he leave a contact number?'

'Sorry! There wasn't time.'

David thought of trying to check if the call could be traced but before he could pick up the phone again, it began to ring and Asleena stretched past him. David was aware of the closeness of her shapely body but he stepped aside.

He saw Asleena's eyebrow rise fractionally as she noticed his discretion. She laughed silently and then turned away.

'Good afternoon! Toby Naughton's office. Pardon? No, I'm afraid he isn't available today. Would you like to make an appointment?'

David snorted in annoyance and stalked back to his own office. He glanced at the appointments for the rest of the day. Only one more. He'd see to that and then finish early. He'd take the back-up discs home again and spend the evening going through them with the proverbial toothcomb.

He picked up the discs to slip into his briefcase but paused with them still in his hand. The image of Sue Anders flooded into his mind, her long glossy hair swinging tantalisingly just out of reach. He rationalised a longing to see her again with the thought that he needed to check out her story. Pastor Jacob was a good judge of character.

Hmm! He slowly tapped his left hand with the discs. It was a while since he had called at The Sheepfold. He knew he was welcome there any time and a taste of Bridget's cooking always did him good.

He lifted the phone. 'Order two dozen chickens from Pannir Selvan, will you, Ko? Yes, ask them to be ready for collection in a cool box by five-thirty. Thanks, Ko.'

His spontaneous change of plan put a fresh vigour into him and he was in a much happier frame of mind when he drew up outside The Sheepfold just before six o'clock. Bridget asked the older girls who were helping to prepare the meal to carry on and received David with a welcoming hug.

David sniffed the aromas of cooking. 'What's on the menu today?'

'Curried vegetables with rice.' She nodded towards the opened cool box.

'You should have come tomorrow. We'll be having Ayam Goreng Berjintan.'

'Don't tempt me — I might take you up on it. Memories of your stir-fried cumin chicken spoils me for anything else!'

'Then, come again, David. You will be very welcome. The boys love to see you. Why don't you come earlier and play football with them?'

'I'm very busy at work,' he regretfully excused himself, ' . . . but, why not? I can work later. You're on, Bridget!' He patted his flat stomach. 'Your cooking will add inches to my waistline, you know!'

'There's not much chance of that, the hours you work. Now, what did you think of Amu's friend? She's a lovely girl, isn't she? Like you, she has a giving heart.' She eyed him speculatively. 'And quite unattached, as you westerners say!'

David laughed, marvelling that Bridget should bring up the very subject he had come to discuss and wondering at the same time, why his heart was suddenly beating faster. 'I'm far too busy to be looking for a wife!' he parried. 'No woman would put up with the hours I work.'

Bridget smiled as she shrugged her shoulders. 'A woman in love will put up with a lot worse than long hours.'

After talking briefly about Sue and her years of friendship by letter with Amu, David left Bridget to oversee the rest of the cooking and went in search of Jacob. An easy camaraderie had built between them during their two years of friendship, and the two men chatted easily.

He was wondering when he would see Sue, and suddenly, there she was, surrounded by a group of girls who were engaging her in lively conversation.

As he watched, he saw her turn in his direction and saw her body freeze for moment as she looked over the heads of the girls towards him. What was she thinking? Did she despise him for his earlier suspicious attitude? He hoped not, at least, not irrevocably.

He tried to convince himself that it didn't matter, but wasn't successful. It did matter. Years of self-training enabled him to keep his face impassive as he quietly excused himself from Jacob and walked towards her. He saw her murmur something to the girls and they all turned towards him.

'Mr David! Mr David!' the girls shrieked joyfully. He was gratified to see that their faces lit up as they recognised him and they all came running over. That should inform her that not everyone thought him to be something on a par with the pantomime ogre, as she no doubt thought.

He greeted the girls warmly with his accustomed friendliness, but his mind was only half on the task. As he touched outstretched hands, patted shoulders, murmured greetings, his eyes strayed to over their heads.

Sue had recovered her poise and was sauntering towards him, smiling politely.

'Miss Anders.' David smiled, unsure

whether to hold out his hand or merely nod.

'Mr Blake.'

Despite his earlier indecision, he impulsively held out his hand. Sue hesitated only fractionally before she placed her hand in his.

'How do you do?' she asked politely. Her eyes met his frankly and seemed to contain a hint of challenge. They were dark brown, the colour of dark chocolate and seemed to be of infinitive depth.

With a start, David realised that he felt as though he were drowning in them and it was only when the notion reached his level of consciousness that he was able to dismiss it as nonsense. He shook his head and said lightly. 'We meet again.'

'Yes,' Sue agreed, smiling faintly.

David inwardly grimaced. She certainly wasn't going to let him off lightly, was she? He swallowed. There was no getting away from it. 'I think I owe you an apology,' he offered hopefully. 'I'm sorry.'

A gurgle of laughter exploded from Sue. 'I'm sorry, too. I should have tried harder to let you know what we'd planned. Quits?'

Relief swept through him. 'Yes, quits.'

'Then may I have my hand back, please?'

'What?' He glanced down, to see, once more, her hand clasped in his. 'Oh! I'm sorry.' He resisted the impulse to stroke the fingers of his left hand along it and, regretfully, he let it go.

'Do you think we should start again?' Sue queried, her eyes full of laughter.

'What a good idea! Tell me, how do you like it here?'

'Is that Malaysia, Kuala Lumpur or The Sheepfold?'

'Whichever you choose, though I meant The Sheepfold.'

Sue gazed around, her head nodding. 'I like it. It's not what I expected. It's so much more relaxed and the children seem very happy. Very different from . . . ' She paused as if unsure how to go on.

' . . . the stereotyped orphanage?'
David suggested.

'Well, yes. And Bridget tells me they don't get any government funding. I don't know how they manage.'

'They live by faith and trust in God's love for them and the children. You will hear them testify that He has never let them down. They always have food to eat and clothes to wear.'

'And different people donate goods and raise money.'

'That's right.'

'Like you?'

David felt embarrassed. He shrugged. 'I do a little.'

They continued to talk lightly throughout the ensuing meal, and it was only pressure of the necessary work on Raju Razak's account that forced David to leave when he did. 'You don't have to come along to clean my apartment, Sue,' he said as they parted. 'Amu won't lose her job, she was never in danger of doing so. Get out and about and enjoy your holiday.'

Sue shook her head. 'I don't mind doing Amu's job. Amu is very proud. She feels it badly enough that I am doing her job, but if no-one were doing it, she would feel compelled to give in her notice.'

He grinned back, happy to feel so relaxed in her presence. 'Well, at least bring your swimwear and make use of the pool,' he suggested, wishing he might have the time to join her but knowing it to be unlikely in the current frenzy of work activity.

'Oh, and you'll need these.' He drew Amu's key and card out of his hip pocket and held them just out of Sue's reach, laughing as she reached up for them. 'There's a price on them,' he warned.

'Oh, yes? And what might that be?'

'A dinner date. Agreed?'

He held his breath, as Sue considered the point, trying in vain to prepare himself for a refusal as he saw various emotions flicker across her face. He felt sure she was going to make an excuse, but she didn't. Sue shrugged and then grinned. 'OK! You're on. When?'

'My first free evening!'

She seemed disappointed, and then resigned.

'I'm sorry I can't do better than that,' he hastened to add. 'It's 'end-of-year' time in the accounting world. I'm going back to my apartment to work right now.'

Sue nodded. 'OK, you're forgiven. I worked for an accountancy firm in Manchester so I know all about the end-of-year-madness!'

David felt extremely light-headed as he drove back to the city centre, thinking over the time he spent with Sue. With a lift in his heart he remembered he had promised to play football with the boys the following afternoon. He felt a glow of anticipation flow through him with the hope that he would probably see her then. He couldn't wait.

He had only just entered his apartment when the telephone rang. As he paused to lock the door, the answer phone clicked on. The first two syllables of the male caller had him sprinting across the room. He snatched up the phone.

'Toby? At last! Where on earth are you?'

'David! Glad to have caught you. What's all this I hear from Asleena? You know I don't like anybody interfering with my clients. Got to build up trust with them, David, my boy. You don't do that passing them on.'

David couldn't believe what he was hearing. 'I'm not interfering, Toby. Raju Razak's tax return is overdue and there's an error in it somewhere. It's over three hundred thousand dollars out of line. It can't be submitted until the error is rectified.'

'Nonsense, David. You've obviously misplaced a few decimal points. Easy to do, my boy! But leave it until I get back, eh?'

David hesitated. Could it be a simple matter of inaccurate recording? It was possible. But why hadn't he detected the error? And it wasn't only that. 'And what about this merger, Toby? Didn't it occur to you to bring me into the picture?'

'What's that, David? Can't hear you too clearly!'

'About the merger deal. How far along has it gone?'

'I'm not keen on it, David,' Toby's voice crackled. 'We'll lose our independence, have to dance to someone else's tune. Leave it to me, David.'

'But when are you coming back, Toby? Where are you? Give me your number, then I can get back to you.'

'Can't hear you, David. Look, leave well alone until I get back, will you? I'll sort it out. I know where to call in a few favours . . . back . . . two days.'

The line went dead. David stared perplexedly at the receiver in his hand. He knew no more than he did before Toby's call, but one thing was clear, Toby knew far more about what was going on in the office than he did.

Someone, probably Asleena, was talking to him. But who contacted whom? Asleena to Toby? Or Toby to Asleena?

Whichever, he wasn't going to sit around and wait for the business to collapse beneath them. He switched on his computer and inserted the back-up disc, clicked on to the appropriate file and began to scroll down the screen.

6

Sue felt herself dragged out of sleep by the strong sunshine and young voices chattering outside. She groaned. Late again! Memories of the previous evening floated into her mind and she sank back against her pillow to savour them properly.

David was nice when he relaxed. She was glad she was going to see him again, if it ever came about, she reminded herself. 'My first free evening,' could be any time in the far distant future.

She almost didn't take her swimwear. For all David had said about using the pool, she wasn't sure.

The memory of the inviting-looking pool five floors down from his living-room window won the day, and she wrapped her bikini into a towel, popped her shampoo and hairbrush into her bag and waved a casual farewell to Bridget.

David arrived outside the office-block which held the premises of Naughton, Naughton & Blake wishing he had been able to take a day off, and wondered if Sue would take up his suggestion of taking her swimming things.

As he travelled up in the lift, he allowed his mind to wander and he imagined Sue's slim figure diving into the pool. She would slice into the water without a splash, he was certain, and she would languorously swim with the crawl stroke across the pool. He was imagining Sue shaking the water out of her hair and eyes when he walked into the outer office to find Ko dabbing her eyes with a handkerchief.

'Now, Ko, whatever is upsetting you? A tiff with your young man, is it?' he asked compassionately, pausing by her desk.

'No, no, sir. It is Asleena.' She apprehensively looked towards the inner-officer door. 'She says she will give me my notice to leave if I do not give her the keys to your filing cabinet. I know I shouldn't have but . . . '

David's attention snapped into first gear. 'And she is in my office right now?'

'Yes, sir. I'm sorry. I didn't know what else to do.'

'Don't worry about it, Ko. I'll deal with it.' Pressing his lips into a firm line he strode into his office, thoroughly irritated by Asleena's high-handedness. He was gratified to see Asleena's usual poise slip a few notches as she turned to see who had entered the room. He took positive delight in drawling, 'Good morning, Asleena. Is there something I can help you with?'

'Oh! Er . . . good morning. I was just . . . er . . . I needed . . . That is Toby said . . . '

'Really? And what did Toby say? That you can demand my personal keys from my secretary and take confidential information from my files?'

'Yes, that is, no. I mean . . . ' Her uncertainty was replaced by a show of defiance. 'Well, you demanded information from Toby's confidential files.'

'I am a partner, Asleena. You are Toby's secretary. Did Toby put you up to this? What exactly does he want?'

'He wants the files back again. He says you are overstepping the mark. They are his clients, not yours and they aren't happy with your interference.'

'And just how does Toby know that his clients are unhappy? Have they got a direct line to him, wherever he's hiding himself?'

'No, of course not, and he isn't hiding. He wants to get back as much as you want him to.'

'So, it's you who is passing on the information? What's the phone number, Asleena? I think you had better give it to me, don't you?'

'I haven't got it,' she replied defiantly. 'Toby gets in touch with me. And it's my job to do as he asks.'

David sighed in exasperation. 'Yes, maybe it is, but the way the things are going, half of our clients aren't going to be able to send off their tax returns by the closing date and they'll run into penalties. They won't exactly be very happy about that, either. Will they?'

'Toby will be back. He said so.'

'I can't risk it, Asleena. There's too much at stake, so put those files back on my desk and . . . ' He paused thoughtfully. 'I want Toby's keys and access to his computer. This needs sorting and I insist on doing it now.'

'You can't! I'll tell Toby the next time he phones!'

David laughed harshly. 'Good! It might get him home again. The keys and the files, Asleena. Now!'

With a tightening of her lips, Asleena swung out of the office and marched angrily into Toby's office. She rummaged in a drawer and flung a bunch of keys on to the desk top. 'The computer is switched on. I won't help you! You've got his password. You'd better get on with it.'

She watched as David moved over to the filing cabinet and began to select some of the files and added, 'I hope you realise just how confidential those files are. They are not to leave these premises.'

'Don't worry,' David assured her, hoping he was choosing the relevant files. 'I'll put them back in Toby's filing cabinet before I leave.'

'You realise, of course, that Toby will probably dissolve the partnership?' Asleena said spitefully.

David smiled coldly. 'And, do you know, Asleena, I really don't care?'

She snatched up her bag and flounced out of the office. David heard her say something cattily to Ko as she passed through the outer office, followed by a slam of the outer door.

★ ★ ★

Sue spent hardly an hour tidying David's apartment. He hadn't been in for more than a few hours. That done, she changed into her bikini, wrapped a blue chiffon sarong around her hips and went down to the swimming pool. The wall of heat still took her by surprise as she stepped outside and it was a wonderful relief to dive into the pool and swim up and down in the cool water. A number of residents were already enjoying the facility but none made any move to engage her in conversation, of which she was thankful.

She relaxed for a while on one of the loungers but, conscious of other things she meant to do, she made her way back to the apartment to shower and change before leaving just past mid-day.

Now more aware of the local geography, she sauntered through the park past where a new conference centre was being under construction.

It was a relief to step into the KLCC building and she enjoyed spending time in the brightly-lit shopping mall, choosing a good selection of hair accessories for the teenage girls at the orphanage. Not wanting to leave out the younger children, she bought a number of colouring books and crayons, regretfully leaving the older boys until a later date, not knowing what they would like.

Bemused by the range of café bars, she chose one advertising Malaysian cuisine, and ordered honey sesame prawns with a salad for her lunch, which she thoughtfully enjoyed. She then made her way to Aunt Rathi's apartment and spent a couple of hours with Amu, discussing her wedding plans and sweet-talking Aunt Rathi, who was now able to sit up in bed, propped up on some pillows.

Sue had taken her a small bowl of fruit and it seemed to please her. She admitted with seeming reluctance that she was feeling a bit better and, yes maybe Amu could spend a few hours with Sue one day soon.

'Amu needs you well and strong for her wedding day, especially after all your hard work helping her to plan it all. It would be a shame to have to miss it, wouldn't it?'

'Miss the wedding? After I have spent many hours of worry over it?' Aunt Rathi sounded surprised. 'I cannot miss the wedding. It is as if she is my daughter, not merely my niece.'

When Sue got in the taxi she had booked, the sky suddenly darkened and the downpour of rain began, accompanied by spectacular zig-zagging streaks of lightning and loud claps of thunder. She was glad she wasn't driving and having to cope with a third of a metre of water gushing along the roads.

'This happens each day!' her driver cheerfully told her. 'It finish soon.'

The storm passed over and the sun was dispersing the clouds by the time Sue arrived at the orphanage. The girls were delighted with the hair ornaments and, except for those on the duty roster that day, they spent the time between finishing lessons and the evening meal experimenting with different hair styles.

When they passed the games field on their way to the dining-room, a disgruntled group of boys were trailing from the field discontentedly passing the football from one to the other, looking anything but exhilarated after a good game.

'What's the matter?' one of the girls called out to them.

'He didn't come!'

'Who didn't?'

'Mr David. He said he would come and play football with us today.'

The girls looked at Sue, as if expecting her to have an explanation but she shrugged her shoulders.

Bridget confirmed the boys' expectations. 'It's not like David to promise something and not to do it,' she mused. 'Something must have happened to prevent him coming. He'll be in touch, I'm sure.'

However, there was no word from him, and Sue set off to his apartment the following day wondering what had happened to cause him to break his word to the boys. His bed had been slept in but apart from that, nothing seemed to have been moved since she had left the previous day.

As she set about tidying the apartment, her inbred insecurities surfaced and she found herself cynically thinking that 'let-downs' were only to be expected. 'Don't rely on anyone!' had been her motto for so long.

David had spent a restless night. Perturbed by the discrepancies he had begun to find in the various 'extra' confidential files he had taken from Toby's office and the files on the computer, he had made copies of all the files in his possession and taken them home, stopping only for a hasty snack in a street café. Once back in his apartment, he continued to work into the early hours of the morning.

Having twice fallen asleep at his desk, he snatched a few hours sleep, but had woken early and continued with the work. When he realised that it was after nine o'clock, he hurriedly slipped the file he was working on into his briefcase and high-tailed it through the park to his office block.

David was finding it hard to believe the discrepancies that were surfacing. Musing on this, when the lift stopped at his floor, it took him a second or two to take in what confronted him. Long water-hoses were trailing across the landing and there was a bustle of activity never seen before. The fact that they were in firemen's uniform hadn't really sunk in when he noticed Ko standing just outside the doorway of the office, literally wringing her hands.

'Oh, sir, sir,' she wailed. 'It is ruined! Everything is quite ruined!'

'What is ruined, Ko? What on earth is happening?'

'Mr Blake?' A fireman with a clipboard in his hand had come out of the office and was looking questioningly at David.

'Yes,' David agreed, his mind whirling. Do you mind telling me what's going on?'

'It seems that you've been the victim of an arson attack, Mr Blake. Could you tell me at what time you left the office building last evening?'

7

David looked blankly at the fire officer's face. 'An arson attack? Here? But why? How? I mean, the whole building hasn't been affected, has it?'

He tried to push past the man, intent on seeing the extent of the damage, but another man blocked his way, flicking out his police rank identity card.

'Mr Blake? If you will just answer some questions before we let you have access to your office, sir. At what time did you leave the building last evening, sir?'

'Er . . . it was late. About half-past ten, I think.'

'Was anyone else still here?'

David shook his head. 'Not in the office. There may have been others in any of the other offices, but I didn't see anyone.'

'Do you usually work so late on your own?'

'Not often. It happens, though, especially at this time of year, with my partner being away, too.'

'The business going well, is it? No sign of problems of any kind?'

'No!'

As he said it, David queried his own emphatic denial and he knew that the hesitation had sounded in his voice.

'Are you sure, sir? No matters of dissention between you and your senior partner . . . er . . . Toby Naughton, isn't it?'

David's eyes narrowed, wondering what the man was getting at. The only person who knew about the discord between himself and Toby was Asleena. What had she been saying? 'Nothing out of the ordinary,' he said coolly, thankful that he was adept at concealing his true feelings.

'Where is Mr Naughton?'

'Unfortunately, he suffered a road traffic accident whilst on holiday recently and hasn't yet returned,' David temporised, irritated once more at Toby for not telling him where he was. 'He is due back any day, now. His secretary should be able to give you any details. Is she here?'

'We have spoken to Miss Mawan. She has been very communicative.'

David kept his face from betraying his wry thought of, *I bet she has*, and decided to try to bring the interview to an end. 'If that is all, may I be allowed inside now? I would like to see what damage there has been done.'

'All in good time, Mr Blake . . . when we have finished taking fingerprints and the fire crew have ascertained the cause of the fire and where it started.'

It was another twenty minutes before David was allowed into the offices and was appalled by the devastation. The computers had melted from the heat and the office furniture was now nothing but blackened pieces of wood. The windows had withstood the heat but were blackened by the smoke and the metal filing cabinets were twisted out of all recognition, their contents burned to ashes.

'Fortunately, the sprinkler system must have switched on immediately and put out the fire before it spread to other offices,' the fire officer was saying as David stared around.

David shook his head in disbelief. Everything had been in order when he had left the building last evening and was now totally destroyed. He ran a hand backwards across the crown of his head.

'How did they get in?' he asked.

'They?' repeated the police officer, his eyebrow raised.

'Whoever did it? He? She? They?' David snapped. 'I locked the doors securely when I left last night. Whoever did it must have broken in!'

'The outer door shows no sign of forced entry. Who has a key beside yourself?'

David glanced over to where Asleena was busily poking into the charred ashes of the filing cabinet. 'Three others have keys to the outer door. My partner, Toby Naughton, Miss Mawan and my secretary, Ko Siew Mei. My secretary has a key to my office. We others have keys to both offices. What are you implying?'

The officer raised his eyebrow but refused to comment. It didn't need a genius to work it out, David thought wryly. He was saying it was an inside job, and all he knew was that it wasn't him.

Eventually, cautioning David and Asleena not to leave the city, the fire and police officers left them. David faced Asleena.

'Well?' he demanded.

Asleena faced him coolly. 'It has nothing to do with me.'

'Which leaves Toby!'

'Nonsense! Toby isn't even in the country.'

'So you would have me believe! The trouble is, Asleena, I don't know what to believe any more!'

'What are you planning to do now?'

David sighed, glancing around. 'There's not much I can do. I might just poke around a bit, though I don't suppose there's anything new left to discover. What about you?'

Asleena shrugged. 'I've seen all there is to see. I'm going home. You know where to contact me if you need to. No doubt Toby will be in touch. He'll be devastated, poor man!'

David looked sceptical but spoke in a neutral voice. 'I'm sure he will. Still, it could be worse. At least I took all the back-up discs and copies of some of the files home with me last night. We could have been completely wiped out of business!'

Asleena's glance dropped to the slender briefcase still held in his left hand. 'All the files?'

'No. Just the ones I was working on. The rest should be on the discs, shouldn't they? I presume all of Toby's business is on the discs?'

'Of course!' Asleena replied quickly.

'How competent of you, David. Toby will be pleased. If you've got the files in your briefcase, maybe I can take them somewhere and get them copied? That will be something for Toby to start to work on when he gets back.'

'Sorry, Asleena. I didn't bring them with me. I intend to work on them at home.'

'There's really no need. Toby will be back today or tomorrow.'

'Good. Do let me know if he gets in touch, won't you, Asleena?'

With a backward, 'Of course!' over her shoulder, Asleena departed, leaving David almost in silence.

Almost, but not quite. David became aware of the sound of sobbing from the outer office, where he discovered Ko huddled on the chair behind her desk. 'At least no-one was hurt, Ko,' he said, patting her shoulders in an attempt to comfort her.

'Not yet, Mr Blake, but I am frightened. Miss Asleena, she tells me to take care.'

'Take care of what . . . or whom?'

Ko shook her head. 'I don't know, but she looked towards you.'

David almost laughed, but refrained. He didn't feel particularly humorous. 'And are you afraid of me, Ko?'

Ko reddened. 'No, sir, but I am afraid,' she whispered. 'I . . . I do not wish to work here, or anywhere with you. Not until it is settled.'

'It's all right, Ko. I understand,' David said gently. 'I don't know what's going to happen, anyway. If you go after another job, I'll give you a good reference. If things get sorted out, I'll let you know. OK?'

After Ko had gone, David's shoulders slumped. Within three days, his life had turned inside out. His business was almost destroyed, his partner was acting with uncomprehending deviousness, and he was under suspicion of arson.

★ ★ ★

Sue had been for a swim and was in the bedroom towelling dry her hair when she heard the door to the apartment open. Thinking it was David, she hastily made sure David's borrowed bathrobe was securely fastened and wrapped the towel around her hair, and then went to the doorway into the living-room.

No-one was there.

Then she saw that the light was on in the small windowless room that David used as his office. She knew she hadn't left it on earlier when she had tidied in there, so she went to say, 'Hello.'

It wasn't David at all. It was a beautiful, well-groomed Malaysian woman. Her sleek black hair was drawn back into a pleat, emphasising her beautiful cheekbones. She was bending over the desk, flicking through a pile of papers that were in a tray.

At the sound of Sue's startled exclamation, the woman straightened. She seemed equally startled to see Sue and her eyebrows rose dramatically.

'Who are you?' Sue asked.

The woman looked her up and down, making Sue feel uncomfortable. 'I might ask you the same thing!' the woman drawled. 'David has certainly kept quiet about you!'

'It's not what you think. I'm ... ' Remembering she didn't have a work permit, she quickly changed her words to, ' . . . a guest.'

The woman's eyebrows remained raised as she flicked her eyes up and down Sue's towelling-robed figure again. 'Well, I'm his secretary and he has sent me to get these papers so, if it's all the same with you, I'll leave you to do whatever you're doing.'

She scooped up the thick sheaf of papers and opened the rather large leather bag than hung from her shoulder.

Before she could drop them inside, something made Sue step forward and take hold of the papers, too. She had worked in an accountant's office for two years and this seemed too casual a way to have important papers collected.

David knew that she was likely to still be in his apartment. Why hadn't he telephoned to let her know his secretary was coming for the papers?

'Let go of them!' the woman hissed, trying to jerk them out of Sue's hands.

Sue held on. There was a chance she was about to make a fool of herself, but if that were so, she knew she had good business practice behind her.

'I'd like to check with David that you are a bonafide messenger. It won't take a minute. See, his office number is on the board.' Sue nodded towards the pinboard where various labels were pinned.

'Really!' the woman exclaimed. 'Who do you think you are? How else would I know about the papers if David hadn't sent me? Stop being a silly girl and let me get on with my job!'

'Then, let's make the phone call!'

Sue thought the woman was about to argue further but, instead, she simply shrugged and said, 'Oh, very well! If you insist!' and let go of the papers.

As Sue turned to pick up the phone, the woman grabbed the papers again and, pushing Sue against the wall, rushed out of the room.

Sue was slightly winded. The towel had fallen from her head, leaving her dishevelled hair tumbling about her face. She rushed after the woman, catching up with her by the outer door to the apartment. The papers were now in the woman's bag and she was about to open the door. Sue grabbed hold of the shoulder strap, hauling the bag off her shoulder.

The strap was still around the woman's arm and the two of them struggled to release it from the other.

'Let go, you fool!' the woman shouted, aiming her free hand at Sue's head.

Sue ducked and only received a glancing blow, but it sent her off balance. Another tug from the woman would have won the tussle but, before she could act, the apartment door opened against her back and David stood framed in the doorway.

'What on earth is going on?' he exclaimed. 'Asleena! What are you doing here? What's happening? Are you all right, Sue?'

Sue's heart sank. David obviously knew the woman. Had she indeed made a fool of herself? But a glance at the woman's face revealed that she wasn't happy at David's intervention.

Emboldened by that, Sue said, 'She said she is your secretary and has taken some of your papers. They are in her bag.'

David looked sharply at the silent but furious woman. 'Don't you think this is taking things a bit too far, Asleena? Hand them over!'

'They're Toby's papers!' Asleena said tightly.

'They're mine until he returns! I want them back!'

He held out his hand. Asleena faced him defiantly but must have realised that she was in no position to defy his command. With ill grace, she pulled the papers out of her bag and thrust them at him.

'You're a fool, David!' she said bitterly. 'You should have kept your nose out of it! You'll be sorry!'

Asleena turned to go. Before she stepped out of the apartment, she looked back over her shoulder. 'Toby will be furious! You will ruin him! He won't forget it!' She pulled the door behind her and it slammed into place.

David stared at the closed door, looking puzzled by her parting words. He dropped his glance to the papers in his hands and then back towards the door.

'What was all that about?' Sue asked quietly.

David looked up sharply, as if he had only just remembered she was there. 'Sue! Are you all right? I'm so sorry you've got caught up in this!'

He immediately put the papers on a large cupboard opposite the door and enveloped her in his arms. His arms felt strong and Sue relaxed against his body. She hadn't realised how shaken she was until it was over. Grappling over a bag with such a well-groomed woman seemed such a ludicrous thing to have happened! 'Are you all right?' David repeated, holding her slightly away from him so that he could see her face.

'I'd never forgive myself if you'd got hurt in all this!' he murmured against her hair. 'Thank goodness you were still here, though!'

He held her firmly for a few moments, until Sue felt his strength calming her trembling limbs. Much as she was enjoying being held so closely to him, it suddenly seemed embarrassing to her and she felt her body go tense again.

David drew back a little, though still holding her arms. 'Come on and sit down,' he suggested. 'Let me make a drink for you. What d'you want? Tea? Coffee?'

'Is she really your secretary?' she asked. 'She said she was, but something didn't seem right.'

'She's my partner's secretary. Toby Naughton. He's away at the moment but due back any day. Asleena had no authority to come here and take those papers. I shouldn't have told her they were here. I should have let her think they were destroyed in the fire.'

'Fire? What fire?'

'Our whole office was destroyed by fire last night. All our files, except those I've got here, our computers, the lot!'

'Oh, no! How did the fire start? Was it accidental? Or . . . ?' Her voice tailed away as she thought of the implications the alternative offered.

From the set of his jaw, Sue could tell that the alternatives weren't lost to David, either. For a moment or two, he seemed undecided what to say. Then, she saw his face tighten and, when he spoke, it was quite brisk. 'Look! I don't want you getting mixed up in all this. Let me make that drink and then you'd best be on your way!'

8

David's abrupt pulling down the shutters over the affair, hit Sue like a blow. She hadn't been seeking information that she had no right to. Her query arose from curiosity, nothing more.

Hiding the rejections she was feeling, she pulled the towelling robe tightly across her body and got to her feet. 'I'll go and get dressed then,' she said quickly and thankfully escaped to the privacy of David's bedroom.

She closed the door and leaned back against it, realising that her legs, her whole body in fact, was trembling again. She couldn't deny, not even to herself, that she was undoubtedly attracted to him. And now he had told her to go.

The memory of being held in his arms and feeling his breath against her hair sent shivers of delight running through her and her throat constricted painfully as she closed her eyes in an attempt to savour the sensation once more. His touch electrified her. Didn't he feel the same?

Sadly she shook her head. He wouldn't be so quick to get rid of her, if he did. It was just her nonsensical longing to be loved that made her react the way she did. For a moment, when he had held her in his arms, it had seemed as though he cared about what might have happened to her, but it must have been no more than passing gratitude for her having foiled Asleena's attempt to remove the papers.

Taking a few deep breaths to steady herself, Sue quickly dressed. Her hair was dry now and she ran her brush through it a few times and tucked some strands behind her ears to keep it from falling over her face. She faced herself in the long mirror on a wardrobe door and straightened her shoulders.

David had made a cup of coffee, which she gratefully drank, but felt slightly on edge as they made small talk for a few minutes. She could sense that he wanted to get on with some work and she was relieved when the opportunity came for her to make her excuses to leave.

She tried to shake off the melancholy mood as she left the building and sauntered through the park towards the KLCC. It was a peaceful place, rich with exotic plants and a beautiful water feature with a medley of fountains that shone like thousands of cascading diamonds, each one reflecting the light from the sun. That, and the crystal effect of the magnificent twin towers, took her breath away and it was with a much lighter heart that she sought out a pleasant café bar where she would eat her lunch.

She determinedly thrust away the mental image of David's smiling face and the tantalising memory of the touch of his hand. The fickleness of a man she had known for such a sort time was not going to ruin her holiday!

England seemed a long way away but she wasn't homesick. There was no-one there to miss, nor to miss her, and she was falling in love with this beautiful city and its equally beautiful happy, smiling people. She felt she was almost over the jetlag and was acclimatising to the constant heat.

Even the daily afternoon downpour didn't dampen her enthusiasm for this tropical land. The rain freshened the air and everywhere dried so quickly afterwards that it was hardly more than a minor inconvenience.

The sky was still clear blue when she emerged from the KLCC and she drank in the sheer exuberance of it, the delight on her face raising a smile on many a passer-by.

She was beginning to know her way around the city centre now and it wasn't long before she picked up a taxi to take her to Amu's home. It was only as she settled back in the rear seat of the taxi that she realised that the hairs on the back of her neck were prickling and she twisted round to look through the rear window.

Her eyes swept back and forth but she couldn't see anything amiss. She slowly twisted back again and leaned back in the seat, her peace of mind unexpectedly thoroughly shaken.

A few nervous glances over her shoulder throughout the short journey showed nothing to be alarmed at, but she remained apprehensive. She paid the taxi driver whilst still inside and looked around to make sure no cars were slowly cruising past when she alighted from the taxi. She hurried across the water buffalo grass to the entrance of the apartments and, again, checked over her shoulder before she closed the door behind her.

Satisfied that it was all in her imagination, she didn't mention her apprehension to Amu and she was careful to give her friend a played-down version of the fire at the offices not wanting to be guilty of over-dramatising the event. David hadn't given her any details anyway and she was sure he would want her to be discreet about it.

Used as she was to working in an accountancy office, discretion was second nature to her. The whole incident was part of his business life, whilst Amu was part of his domestic arrangements. Consequently, she said nothing about Asleena's visit either.

Instead, she readily listened to more of Amu's wedding plans and was pleased when Aunt Rathi came into the sitting-room and said that she was feeling much better.

Even though Sue was pleased, she experienced a strange pang in her stomach. She realised it was because there was the possibility of Amu soon being able to return to her job at David's apartment, which meant she would no longer have the occasional opportunity of seeing David there, and was immediately ashamed at her selfishness. How could she!

Amu seemed surprised when her aunt appeared in the room and

hurriedly made sure that the older woman was seated comfortably.

Sue smiled to herself when Aunt Rathi said, 'You're a good girl, Amu.' Maybe her visits had helped Amu's relationship with her aunt?

As usual, Amu escorted Sue to the main road. The sky had clouded over and it was evident that the afternoon storm was coming early today. Even as she hailed a passing taxi, huge drops of rain began to fall.

'Don't linger, Amu,' Sue begged her friend. 'See, that taxi driver has seen me. Run back before you get soaked.' Sue kissed Amu's cheek, pleased at the way the visit had gone.

'See you tomorrow!' She held her small bag over her head in the vain attempt to keep her hair dry and ran forward towards the taxi that was drawing to a stop at the kerb. She pulled open the door and tumbled inside, laughing in her relief to have escaped becoming wet through.

Before she was able to give her

desired destination, the taxi set off, entering the traffic flow with the habitual disregard of Kuala Lumpur drivers, causing Sue to be flung back against the rear seat. Still not truly alarmed she tapped on the glass partition to gain the driver's attention in order to give him her destination, but he took no notice.

They were travelling speedily along the highway, the rain pouring in streams down the windows, giving a distorted image of the world outside. All she could see were the distorted shapes of other vehicles and buildings.

Who was he? Where was he taking her? What did he want of her? She frantically rapped on the glass partition again, beginning to feel extremely alarmed. No-one knew where she was and no-one would miss her until Pastor Jacob or Bridget realised that she hadn't returned.

She cast her mind back to her earlier uneasiness, her concern that she being followed, and couldn't believe that she had dropped her vigilance and jumped into the first taxi that came along without even checking that the driver could speak English. How stupid could she be?

Fighting to stay in control of her emotions, she had no doubt in her mind that she was being abducted. But, for the life of her, she couldn't think why.

She had to remain calm and think of a way to get out of this. Even as that thought occurred to her, she became aware of the incessant tooting of car horns and she realised that the taxi had come to a virtual standstill, hemmed in on all four sides by other hooting vehicles.

She dived to the left-hand door and yanked the handle. The door flew open and she all but tumbled out into the narrow space between the taxi and the next vehicle. She was ankle deep in rainwater and she was thankful to realise that the customary afternoon flood had come to her aid. The road ahead dipped slightly downwards under an overhead flyover and the accumulated water made progress impossible.

A shout from her driver made her hastily look over the taxi at him as he partly climbed out. He looked as though he were about to rush round the vehicle to grab hold of her but she didn't wait to hear what he had to say or to see what he intended to do.

Clutching her bag to her body, she began to weave in and out of the stranded vehicles running back the way they had come, hoping that the man wouldn't leave his vehicle. She didn't pause until she reckoned she had put a good distance between her and the taxi driver, when she risked a look over her shoulder.

No-one was following her, and when the traffic started moving, her abductor would have no option other than to move with it, taking him farther and farther from her. He must have been simply a hired hand, he wasn't going to abandon his taxi to chase after her.

She was thoroughly soaked, her hair hanging in rats' tails, her thin summer frock clinging to her like a second skin. A few drivers glanced her way but she didn't want any heroic deeds from any of them. Who could she trust? No-one in the near vicinity.

She stood still and looked around. In the distance, she could see the tall Petronas Towers thinly veiled in rain and mist, but how to get there? She didn't want to stay on the road. The downpour never stopped the traffic for more than ten minutes or so and the taxi cab would then be freed to be driven up and down this section whilst the driver searched for her. She was in the suburbs and was in no mood to trust strangers for help.

Her eyes lit upon an overhead structure just as a train zoomed over it. The monorail! That was her answer! Where was the nearest station? Even as she asked herself the question, the train stopped a few hundred metres along the structure to her right, and she could see that the concrete support at that point comprised of more substance than mere supporting pillars. She darted across and quickly left the road behind her.

She met no-one until she neared the steps that led up to the rail-line, and they merely saw her as a would-be passenger caught out in the rain. She was glad to lose herself amongst them and followed the flow up the steps. Many went towards a series of ticket machines and, glancing at the list of stations, she was thankful to see the KLCC listed amongst other destinations, giving a code number and price of the ticket.

A further glance around showed her which side of the platform to stand on. Choosing to stand by a pillar that partly concealed her, she kept watch on the top of the steps in case her driver was still in pursuit, but no-one identifiable appeared.

Even so, she was thankful when the train arrived, gliding silently to a stop just a few metres away. She moved into the group of passengers boarding the train, feeling safer in their midst. Surely no-one would dare to try to abduct her from such a public place.

What if the driver reported her escape and whoever it was guessed that the monorail would be her chosen escape route? Would they guess that she would alight at the KLCC and send someone to apprehend her? A rail-layout with the names of all stations on route was just above her head, but the other station names meant nothing to her.

She knew that she didn't dare risk getting into another taxi and she didn't know who to approach to ask for help, what would she say?

The train drew in the KLCC station before Sue had decided what to do. She didn't want to remain isolated on the platform so she followed the stream of passengers through the exit barrier, down the steps and along a concrete-lined passage, emerging into the shopping mall.

The cool air-conditioning wasn't

enough to dry her clothes and she was beginning to feel the effects of the wet chill. Had she got Pastor Jacob's phone number? No, it would take too long to explain and for him to get to her.

The only person she could think of was David Blake. It would have to be him. Thank goodness she had put the slip of paper with his number on it into her bag when she had been trying to phone him on her first day here.

With eyes warily scanning the crowds, she found a phone booth and dialled the number with trembling fingers. Let him be in! Let him be in!

'Hello?' The sound of his voice made it difficult to hold back a sudden threat of tears but she fought the impulse. If she cried, she wouldn't be able to speak.

'David, it's Sue. Sue Anders.'

'Sue! Great to hear from you! How can I help you?'

'I need your help, David. I'm stranded at the KLCC and I'm soaking wet and I . . . '

'Right! Look, jump into a taxi and I'll meet you at the security gate. I've cancelled all passes, so I'll need . . . '

Her breath caught in her throat. 'I daren't, David! I . . . I think I was abducted, but I escaped . . . and I'm scared to get into another taxi!' She felt stupid and weak but couldn't help it! And if he laughed at her she would burst into tears and she didn't know what she would do then.

He asked sharply, 'Are you safe where you are?'

Sue glanced nervously around her. 'Y . . . yes, I think so. I'm in the shopping mall and there are people about.'

'Which floor are you on?'

She looked around again, more confident now that David's reassuring voice was in her ear. 'I'm not sure, but I can see a Kodak photographic shop.'

'Right, stay there. I'll be with you in five minutes.'

It was slightly more, and it seemed like five hours, but Sue didn't complain. She hadn't planned how she would greet him. If she had, she would have tried to remain cool, calm and in full control of herself.

As it was, the sight of his familiar figure broke through all her reservations and she flung herself into his arms, sobbing, 'David! David! I've been so scared!'

9

It was the second time that day that David had held her in his arms, and this time it felt even better than before.

His voice was murmuring comforting sounds into her hair, and their calming effect gradually soaked through to her agitated mind. She could feel some of the tension drain out of her body and, when David said, 'Come on. Let's get to my car and I'll take you home,' she obediently fell into step at his side and let him lead her like a child down to the basement car park.

He kept his arm around her shoulders and she could feel the warmth and strength of him. He opened the passenger door for her and she gratefully slid into the seat. The air had been warm in the car park and her muscles had relaxed slightly, but now, in the cool air-conditioning of the car, she began to shiver again.

'I'll soon have you home,' David said comfortingly. 'A hot shower and a drink will get you warm again.'

She felt too chilled to hold any conversation but David didn't seem to mind. They went up to the fifth floor in the lift and he unlocked the door to his apartment.

He turned off the air-conditioning and opened the balcony window to let the outside warm air invade the apartment. The rain had ceased now, and the sky was incredibly blue again. Then he gave her a clean towel and left her to have a warm shower.

'Use my bathrobe again, until your dress dries!' he called out to her and, when she eventually emerged, her body warmed by the water and the warm air, he added, 'It looks better on you than it does on me!'

Sue was glad her body had stopped trembling and she was grateful for the mug of coffee that David put into her hands but, when he asked what it had all been about and she began to recount what had happened, her voice broke again and she knew that the shock of it all was still with her.

'Don't worry!' David calmed her. 'You've had a nasty experience and I'm only too sorry that I didn't anticipate it!'

Sue looked at him in surprise. 'What do you mean? It was nothing to do with you, was it? How could it be? There's no connection between us apart from these past few days when I've done your housekeeping.'

'No, but Asleena doesn't know that. She probably thinks we're living together, that I care about you. I think you were abducted to get at me. A 'lever', if you like, to persuade me to give back Toby's papers.'

Sue noticed the words, 'She probably thinks I care about you' and realised sadly that it wasn't true.

'Would you have done?' she asked curiously.

David regarded her seriously. 'Probably,' he answered after a pause. 'Though, not being one to throw in my hand too readily, I would have probably also tried to track you down and rescue you.'

'On your white charger?'

'Of course! Heavily disguised as my dark blue Volvo!' he added.

For a moment Sue relaxed into the friendly banter but the memory of the terrifying car ride thrust itself forward and she instantly sobered. 'I was scared,' she admitted quietly.

Equally soberly, David leaned forward. 'I'm not surprised. Anyone would have been. And, like I said earlier, I'm sorry that I didn't anticipate something like that happening.' He shook his head. 'I just didn't, and that's that!'

'But why should you have done? I don't see . . . '

'Because of what's been happening at work over the past few days. Look, I know I haven't known you very long but I've got to talk about it with someone to try to sort everything out in my mind. You did say you used to work in an accountant's office, didn't you?'

'Yes, I did.'

'Good! I feel, somehow, that you might be just the one to be able to help me sort through it all.'

As David briefly recounted the disturbing events and disclosures of the previous few days, Sue listened with increasing amazement. 'So, what is your partner up to? Falsifying tax returns for some of his clients?'

David nodded. 'That's what it looks like. Of course, I've only been through a few files so far and some seem to be in order. Others, however, show alarming discrepancies.'

'They couldn't just be typing errors, could they?'

'That's what Toby would like me to think. He more or less suggested as much in the one phone call I've had from him. But, if that's all they are, why has he been so desperate to keep the files out of my hands? No, I think he is

135

definitely keeping two sets of books. One set for the taxman and the other for his own records and his clients.'

'So, what are you going to do about it?'

David sighed. 'I've no option, really. If I go along with it, even just ignore it, I would become a party to it. And that I will not do. I worked hard to get into the position I now hold. I'm not going to throw it away.'

'Have you enough proof?'

'Not yet. With all the records destroyed in last night's fire, all I have are these few copies of some of Toby's files and all the back-up discs, and they're as much in my computer as Toby's. There's now no record of Toby's password having been excluded from my scrutiny. I could be held to hold equal responsibility with Toby and liable for prosecution. And Toby's been away for the past two weeks. He could say it has all happened since I was left in charge.'

Sue considered his words. 'No,' she

contradicted. 'Computer boffins can find out when details were first added to a computer.'

David shook his head. 'You're forgetting the fire. Both office computers have been completely destroyed. Unless Toby has the details on another computer at his home, or somewhere else, the only electronic records are here on my computer, and they don't show the fraudulent figures. Those are on these paper copies I made of some of Toby's confidential files.'

'He's bound to have other copies.'

'Yes, but he's not likely to offer them for scrutiny, is he? In fact, once he gets to know what's happened, it's more than likely that he'll get rid of all the incriminating evidence he can get his hands on, or hide it far away from risk of detection.'

'Then, we've got to beat him to it!'

David glanced at her sharply. 'We?'

'It will take for ever on your own. Two of us will do it in half the time.'

'You're sure?'

David's eyes warmed visibly and Sue felt a tingle run through her. When he reached out and touched her hand, she felt an electric current surge through her and she had to fight the urge to lean forward towards him. She sensed that if she did so, he would inevitably kiss her and, whereas she somehow knew it would be the most delightful kiss she had ever had, she also knew it was only because he was grateful for her offered help, and it could lead to complications he would later regret.

So, she drew her hand away and stood up. 'I think we had better get down to work,' she suggested, feeling a tug of regret in her heart as a flicker of disappointment flitted across David's face.

She was feeling uncomfortably hot. 'Why don't you put the air-conditioning back on whilst I go and get dressed. I'm sure my dress will be dry now.'

It was, and Sue went to put it on, wondering what sadistic emotional torture she had let herself in for. She dressed quickly and, as an after-thought, took a *scrunchie* out of her bag and fastened her hair.

David was already running off printed copies of accounts from the back-up discs when Sue joined him in the small office. She noticed he had changed the font colour to blue.

'That's a good idea,' she complimented him. 'We'll know which copy is which.'

They began to work through the files, finding numerous extra entries in the scanned paper copies. These, they highlighted and grew more and more incredulous as the amounts added up.

'Phew! No wonder Toby didn't want anyone to see those copies. Even from the entries checked so far, he has saved his clients the equivalent of almost a quarter of a million dollars this year alone,' David marvelled.

'And you can bet he's had a good pay-off from the clients concerned. I suppose you realise that this information is pure dynamite,' Sue added soberly, turning to face him.

David's face was equally grave. He nodded slowly. 'I do and I'm wondering what he will do next? Whether or not Asleena has his phone number, he'll have a way of getting in touch with her and she won't hesitate to tell him that the abduction plan failed and that I've still got these copies.'

'If it was him who set up my so-called abduction.'

'I can't think of any other reason. Can you?'

'Not really.' Sue sighed. 'Do you think he'll send someone else here to try to get the papers?'

'I don't know,' he admitted frankly. 'But I don't think so. He's lost the element of surprise and I've changed the locks, anyway, so an intruder would have to break down the door.'

His eyes rested on her for a moment. 'I don't want you to get hurt in all this, though,' he said softly.

He stared blankly, his eyes unfocused for a few minutes and Sue felt an emotional lump come to her throat. He did care for her, at least for her safety. He was a kind, compassionate man, she realised.

She studied his tanned face, memorising each individual feature — the shape of his chin with just the hint of a dimple in it, his nose, the tiny laughter crinkles at the outer corner of his eyes, the way his hair fell slightly forward. She again wished she could smooth it back and run her fingers through its silky softness.

She was drawn out of her reverie when David suddenly said, 'You can't go back to the orphanage tonight. It might put you into too much danger.'

Sue was startled. 'Why not? What danger are you thinking of?'

'He might try to abduct you again. And even if he didn't get you on the journey, you would have led him to The Sheepfold and it's far too vulnerable a place. There are over seventy children there. Any one of them could be taken and held hostage. I can't risk it. Toby has more than just the money at stake. It's his business reputation as well. He wants these papers and discs and I don't think he's going to give in too easily.'

'So, what do I do?'

'You stay here. I'll sleep out here.'

So, she stayed the night. She slept in David's bed and David on one of the sofas in the living-room.

If only she dared to trust him. She felt he liked her but hadn't dared to give him any encouragement to think she reciprocated his feelings. It wouldn't last. Nothing ever did. You gave your heart away, only to lose it forever. And that meant pain and longings that were hard to dispel.

10

They hadn't been working on the remaining files for more than half-an-hour when the telephone rang. David picked it up, giving his name in introduction.

As he listened to the voice at his ear, his face instantly changed and with a gesture to Sue not to talk, he switched on the loudspeaker, mouthing the name, 'Toby.'

' . . . about the fire at the office. I was devastated, old boy! We could go out of business without any records of our clients' business affairs. You haven't got any back-up copies by any chance, have you?'

David leaned back in his chair and threw a cynical glance at Sue. 'As it happens, Toby, I do have some copies but they don't all seem to be up-to-date. Like I said to you the last time you phoned, quite a number have various discrepancies with the written files, so I don't know how much value they will be in the long run.'

'You're not still on about that, are you?' Toby asked with a note of mild irritation in his voice. 'Look I told you, David, they are nothing but typing errors. I'll get them sorted out in no time, once I'm back with you. Look, I'll get in touch with Asleena and ask her to pop around and get them for me. I'll be back in KL by tonight.'

'No, Toby,' David said sharply. 'Asleena has already been round here, as I'm sure you perfectly well know. I'm not letting these papers out of my sight. They need stringent inspection and a convincing explanation, which I'm not sure you'll be able to give. What have you been thinking of, Toby? These papers could be professional suicide, both for you and the business.'

Toby gave a half-laugh. 'Nonsense, old boy! You're reading too much into it!' His voice changed into a hopeful conciliatory tone. 'Look, I can see we need to talk about it face-to-face, David. I've got it covered from all angles. It's a cinch, David.'

'No, Toby. The fraudulent returns have got to be rectified.'

There was a hollow laugh at the other end of the phone line. 'That's not how you make big money, David. Look, I tell you what. I was due to meet Andrew Forbes this evening as soon as I've landed. You remember him? He started his own advisory service a couple of years back. It's all legal, he assures me. Why don't you meet with him this afternoon? Show him the papers, if you like. He'll soon put your mind at rest.'

'I'm not sure, Toby. Look . . . '

'I'll give him a ring and tell him to expect you. Three o'clock this afternoon suit you? At his place, you know, out towards the mountains to the northeast? I'll give you his address, got a pen handy?'

David wrote down the address Toby

dictated to him and, with a breezy farewell, the line went dead.

'What d'you think, Sue?' David asked with a frown. 'I don't see how he can talk this away. Do you?'

Sue shrugged. 'Not according to anything I've ever seen. He sounded pretty certain, though, didn't he?'

'At least he doesn't mind this Andrew Forbes giving the papers a 'going over'. It will give us a second opinion, anyway, won't it?'

'Right. Well, let's get everything listed that we've found so far. You've coded each item to match its counterpart, so we shouldn't have any problem explaining what we're talking about to this Andrew guy.'

'I'm not sure you should come with me. All this has made me realise that I don't really know Toby all that well. I'm not sure I trust him.'

'It's not Toby we're going to see. It's a professional advisor. He'll give us his independent opinion. I'll be able to back up whatever you're saying and be a witness to any advice he gives. Two heads are better than one.'

David gave her a look of appraisal. 'Especially when one of them is yours,' he grinned.

They worked on in companionable rapport to collate everything they had discovered, and then David made them both an omelette for an early lunch, whilst Sue tossed a green salad.

She recognised that he was lightly flirting with her and skilfully parried his teasing moves towards her. She had had enough practice, she reflected, although she had to admit to herself that her resolve to continue was less sure.

After washing the dishes together and tidying away the crockery, David suggested it was time to set out and they left his apartment, David carrying the wad of papers and discs in his briefcase.

Unnerved by the events of the previous day, Sue couldn't help glancing apprehensively around the almost deserted car park in the basement of the apartment block.

'I'll hold on to that,' she said decisively, as David was about to toss the briefcase on to the rear seat, along with his jacket.

As they drove towards the gates, David said, 'Open my briefcase and get out the manila envelope, will you, Sue?'

'What's in it?' Sue asked curiously as she read the address. Her eyebrow lifted at the sight of the bank note clipped to it.

'Our insurance,' David said flatly. He wound down his window and one of the guards came over. 'Has anyone tried to get in without a security pass?' he asked.

'No, sir. We'll continue to keep a look out, though.'

'Thanks.' He held out the envelope. 'Will you hand-deliver this as soon as possible, please? It's very important.' The gates opened and David raised his hand in salute to the security guards as he drove through.

Sue enjoyed the scenery in this

western lowland area of Malaysia and she gazed avidly about her, admiring the traditional wooden Malaysian houses that were now more evident.

'Tell me a little about yourself, Sue,' David's voice invited.

Sue jumped. Her mind had been far away and she felt flustered by his question. 'I . . . er . . . I'm just ordinary,' she stammered. 'You know, went to school, grew up, got a job.'

'No family? Brothers and sisters?'

'No. Only me!' she forced herself to answer lightly. 'How about you?' It was one of the ploys she had developed — to throw back the question. It drew off the heat.

'Well, I'm the same . . . and the opposite.' David said enigmatically, grinning at her confused expression. 'I'm an orphan. Come on, say, 'Aw!' ' he cajoled.

Sue was stunned. She hadn't suspected. But why should she? Orphans didn't look any different . . . on the outside. Only on the inside, she reflected sadly.

'But, don't you mind?' she found herself asking, although she had had no such intention of intruding into his privacy.

'Mind? Why should I? It wasn't intentional on anyone's part and, as I said, although I have no blood relatives, I've got sixty or more adopted brothers and any number of aunts and uncles I still keep in touch with.'

Sue tried to take in this, what was to her, a surprising statement. She realised that David was puzzled by her silent reaction and had prolonged his sideways glance at her face and, almost too late to warn him, she saw a large black car suddenly zoom from nowhere behind them and rapidly draw level.

'Watch out!' she warned sharply, as the car cut across their path.

With an involuntary shout of alarm, David snatched at the steering wheel, trying to avoid the inevitable crash, but he had nowhere to go . . . except off the road and down the now steeply sloping hillside.

It all happened so fast that ordered thought was impossible. Sue was unaware of holding on tightly to the hand-rest by her left hand and hugging the briefcase and her shoulder bag to her chest with her right. Her eyes were fixed straight ahead through the windscreen as David struggled to control their downward plunge, but with little notable success. Trees loomed and were narrowly missed, their branches scraping the windows.

They were going to be killed! She just knew it! David's voice came in gasps and grunts and, when a small cluster of trees loomed directly in their path, he used all his strength to wrench the steering wheel to the right.

The car wheels spun wildly as the car made a ninety-degree turn. Its rear portion continued to spin and crashed with a resounding bang into the trunk of one of the trees, its impact causing both front doors to fly open.

Sue felt her bodyweight forcing her diagonally forward until the jerk of the seatbelt pulled her back against the seat, throwing her head against the head-rest and off again. Stunned by the impact, she was still frozen in immobility when she was aware that David's hand was fumbling at her side and she heard his voice command, 'Get out! Now!'

As David threw himself out at the driver's side, Sue all but tumbled out of the passenger door and began to roll uncontrollably down the hillside.

David rolled as he hit the ground, instinctively protecting his neck and head. He lay winded for a second or two before the urgency of seeing how Sue had fared drove him to his feet.

He darted around the front of the car but she wasn't there. He anxiously swung his gaze down the slope. There she was, crumpled at the base of a tree. Immediately, he began to descend towards her, slipping and slithering down the slope.

It took less than a minute to reach her and his heart was in his mouth as he crouched over her. She looked so limp that he feared the worst had happened and that she was dead, but as he reached out and tentatively touched her cheek, she moaned and tried to move.

'It's all right! Don't move, Sue,' he cautioned, gently stroking her cheek. 'Get your breath back and we'll see how you . . . '

A bang and a roar drowned out his words as his car exploded into flames hurtling pieces of metal into the air. The blast took him off his feet and the heat was unbearable. 'I'll have to drag you away!' he shouted to Sue, hoping he wasn't adding injury to her body as he did so.

By taking her farther down the slope a little, the natural curve of the hillside gave some protection from the heat, and the flames, having leaped upwards after the initial explosion, were now burning low in a molten ball of red, sending trails of acrid black smoke dispersing into the air.

Sue stirred, moaning softly. 'Ooh! My back! What happened?' She struggled to lift up her upper body and leaned on her elbow, seeing David's anxious face close to her own.

'Easy!' he cautioned. 'You might do extra damage.'

She tentatively rolled her shoulders and wriggled her back from side to side. David was crouched on his haunches beside her. 'I think everything is working,' she ventured. 'How about you?'

'I'm OK. Do you think you can make it up to the road? I've heard one car go past but it didn't stop. We're in need of help.'

'What happened?'

'A car forced us off the road. Fortunately, we managed to get out before it exploded. We've been very lucky!'

Sue digested the information, letting it sink in. It had happened so quickly, that she hadn't really registered the sequence of events at the time, but she nodded her head, accepting what he said.

David helped her to her feet and they began to pick their way carefully up the slope, veering away from the smouldering remains of David's car. Sue was glad of his supporting hand and, as he paused to get her balance, she saw a black leather bag on the ground to her left.

'Your briefcase,' she pointed out. 'Thank goodness it's safe! And there's my bag just beyond it.'

The sound of a car engine purring its way up the road intruded into the scene and David slithered back to her side, the briefcase and bag in his hand. 'Get down!' he commanded, pulling her down and lying at her side, his arm across her body.

An image of the black car that had forced them off the road snapped in front of Sue's eyes and she had to blink to force it away. What if the driver had returned?

The car came into view and drew to a stop above them. Its colour was red, Sue was relieved to note, as its driver got out. He was Malaysian and neither of them recognised him, but David shook his head at Sue as she made as if to rise to her feet.

'Daren't risk it!' he whispered. 'Come on! Wriggle backwards into the shrubs. I don't want anyone to know we survived the crash.'

There was no sound of the man coming to look for them and after retreating a few hundred metres, David signalled to Sue to stop.

He levelled his gaze at her, his face serious. 'Tell me honestly, Sue. Do you really think that driver deliberately forced us off the road?'

Sue tried to be as objective as possible as she forced herself to think over those few horrible seconds when she realised that they were going to career down the hillside. 'I'm sure he knew what he was doing. There was absolutely nothing else on the road.

There was ample room for him to overtake and hold his line until he was well-ahead of us. Instead, he cut right on.'

David nodded slowly. 'Like you say, there was plenty of room for him to overtake safely right there. Coming on top of everything else, like it does, it had to be deliberate. The next question is, who was it? And on whose orders?'

'Ha! Well, as to whose orders it was, there's only one person who knew we were going there, isn't there? Toby.'

'And Andrew Forbes.'

Sue pursed her lips. 'Maybe. We've only Toby's word for that.'

'True, but let's keep him in the equation for now. Who else?'

'Asleena? Could she have been the driver, do you think?'

David nodded. 'You're right. She could.'

He silently stared into the distance for a moment, then brought his gaze back to rest on her. There was a light of determination in his grey eyes. 'I want to confront Toby.'

11

Sue stared at him. 'You certainly believe in tackling things head on, don't you?'

David shrugged. 'What's the alternative? Anyway, whatever Toby is up to, I still find it hard to believe he really wants to kill me. I've worked with the man for over two years. I think he just wants to scare me into giving back these papers.'

'Maybe, but we were very fortunate not to get killed back there.'

'Yes, I know. That's why I don't want to lead you into any more danger. I'll meet him on my own. I'll get back to civilisation and then consider what to do.'

The thought of David walking into possible danger on his own made Sue realise that she didn't want him to do anything on his own ever again. She wanted to be at his side, for as long as he was part of her life. If he later chose to leave her, she would face that when it came.

She thought for a minute. 'Why don't we meet him at the airport? He won't do anything there. What time is his plane due?'

'I don't know, and my mobile phone is now a mere bit of melted metal and plastic. So are my wallet, credit cards and keys.'

He gazed back up the mountains with a thoughtful look in his eyes. Sue knew what he was thinking. 'How far are we from Andrew Forbes' house?'

He smiled faintly as he glanced down at her. 'Not far. Another kilometre or so.'

'Then I'm coming with you.'

'No! It's too dangerous.'

'No more for me than for you. In fact it will be less dangerous. There'll be two of us, and I'll be able to back up everything you say. Let's tidy ourselves up. See, I've got some wet-wipes in my bag.'

She opened her bag and took out a small packet of wipes. 'Here you are.'

David took the wipe out of her hand and rubbed it across his face. She chuckled. 'You've missed most of it! Here, give it to me and bend down!'

She took the wipe out of his hand and began to clean his face but her hand slowly came to a halt as she read in David's eyes the longings that were in her own thoughts. She swallowed hard and began again, trying but failing to remain dispassionate about it.

'There!' she tried to say lightly when she had removed the smears of soil and dust, drawing her hand away.

David gently took hold of her hand and held it to his lips. Sue gasped as a frisson of delight rippled through her. Her eyes locked with his and neither of them moved until David said, 'Now your turn.'

He took the packet of wipes from her hand and pulled out another wipe. Still holding eye contact, he gently began to wipe her face.

'You're beautiful,' he said softly. 'You know I've fallen in love with you, don't you?'

'Have you?' she whispered, hardly daring to breathe, feeling a flicker of alarm sweep through her. She felt confused.

Sue knew he was going to kiss her and held her breath. She wanted him to, but felt a sense of panic. What if he were disappointed in her? And then didn't want her? She should tell him to stop before it was too late!

But it was already too late. David lowered his lips to cover hers. They felt soft and warm and as smooth as velvet. Sue found her hands had risen up to clasp his head to hers. The response of her body made her feel quite weak and she knew that if David were to let her go, she would fall to the ground.

But he didn't let go, not at once. He drew back a little and smiled into her eyes. 'I've been wanting to do that since the first time I met you, if I'm honest,' he said with a little laugh. 'Certainly since I found you in my apartment. But you kept holding me at a distance, as if you were afraid of me.'

Sue didn't know what to say. He would think her a fool but she knew she had gone too far to pull back completely. She was going to have to learn to trust him.

'I wasn't afraid of you,' she whispered. 'Just afraid of loving you!'

'Afraid to love?'

She nodded unhappily, looking away. She knew she had to risk ridicule. She had to explain.

'I was afraid because everyone I have ever loved went away. My parents died when I was seven. A neighbour looked after me for a couple of weeks, but then she handed me over to Social Services and I went to a children's home. She never came back to see me. No-one ever came. And it always seemed as though anyone I became friendly with went away. They were adopted or relatives were traced and they took them away.'

David clasped her to him. 'And no-one ever wanted to adopt you?'

'Maybe I didn't try hard enough . . . or maybe I tried too hard. I don't know. I wasn't a pretty child. My hair was too fine and it was always done in tight pigtails, pulled back off my face 'til it hurt. I'd no front teeth and had to wear glasses for a few years. I became known as difficult and people who took me on outings never invited me again.

'I preferred to read or work with numbers. I decided to become top of the class. It was safer. If I worked hard, no-one could beat me.' She laughed humorously. 'I was the class swot! I never went on dates and no-one asked twice!'

'Then I've got to teach you to expect to be loved. I must teach you to reach out and grasp hold of it. Will you let me? Do you trust me?'

Sue nodded. She knew that was what she wanted. She too had known it from the time they first met. It seemed too wonderful to be true, too wonderful to last. The thought of being left without him was too dreadful to bear.

'That's why you must let me come with you,' she pleaded earnestly. 'I'm afraid that, if you go on your own, something bad will happen and you'll never come back!'

David nodded understandingly. 'We'll go together,' he agreed. 'I'll feel safer with you at my side or watching my back.' He hugged her close again and then kissed her deeply.

'Now I've found you,' he said joyously. 'I'll never leave you. We've got the rest of our lives to spend together.

'Now, we'd best get a move on before the afternoon rain comes,' David declared, looking up at the sky. 'I want us to keep off the road just in case whoever it was comes back to check.'

They carefully scrambled back up the hillside and cautiously crossed over the road, preferring to be higher than the road, looking down on it in case anyone came back to look for them.

The trees thinned a little as they

neared the next kampung village. As usual, there were a variety of buildings. David looked for Jalan Pandanus, the name of the road that Toby had given him, and then for the right number.

It was a large, imposing house, set back from the road and built of wood in the traditional Malaysian style. The ground floor was open-plan, with eight-foot high stilts holding up the main frame of the house. There was a central clock with an ornate covered stairway leading up to the main floor and a large *wing* on both sides.

'Right! Shoulders back, here we go,' David murmured in her ear. 'Remember, we think we are here by appointment.'

Sue nervously followed David up a few steps to the door set in the porch and waited anxiously as he rang the bell. The man who opened the door a few minutes later was of Malaysian origin. He bowed politely. 'How may I help you?' he asked in clear English.

'Mr Forbes is expecting us, I believe.'

The man's eyebrow rose frantically,

but he bowed again. 'Your names, sir?'

'David Blake and my assistant, Miss Anders.'

'Please step inside. I'll make enquiries.'

David knew that according to Malaysian code of conduct, he ought to have stayed just inside the porch but he didn't want to lose his advantage of surprise, so he nodded to Sue to follow him and closely followed the manservant up the steps.

He was able to see the visible shock on the faces of the two men and one woman who were seated in the spacious living-room — Andrew Forbes, Asleena Mawan . . . and Toby Naughton.

'David!'

It was Toby whose self-control had slipped and spoke David's name into the tense atmosphere. The manservant bowed and retreated, closing the door again, leaving David and Sue standing just inside the room. Toby's presence took David by surprise but he felt he hadn't betrayed that fact beyond the natural reaction to his senior partner's early return.

'You're back early, Toby. Good flight, was it?' he said innocently, moving forward, drawing Sue with him.

'Er . . . yes, yes. I managed to get an earlier flight at the last minute. Couldn't let the chance slip by, you know.'

David swept his glance over Asleena as he made his quiet response. Her face had gone white and her eyes were wide in disbelief.

'But I . . . You . . . '

Her startled gaze swung from him to Toby and back. 'You were expecting me, weren't you?' David asked artlessly.

Andrew Forbes strode forward, his hands outstretched. 'Yes, yes, David,' he said smoothly. 'It's just that you are a little later than expected. We'd given you up, you know. Er . . . problems on the way, were there?'

'Just a matter of being run off the road by a careless driver,' David said calmly, as if it happened to him frequently.

'But . . . ' Asleena spoke again but instantly stopped, her fingers nervously fluttering near her throat as she intercepted a warning glance from Andrew.

'Good. Good. And your companion?'

Andrew held out his hand towards Sue. 'Miss Sue Anders,' David said in introduction of her.

She instinctively didn't like Andrew Forbes and didn't want to touch his hand but felt compelled to act out the game they had chosen to play, repeating the handshake with Toby.

Asleena merely stared at her with open dislike. Sue returned her stare without rancour, wondering if Asleena's reaction pointed to her being the driver of the car that had run them off the road.

'No harm done, then, eh?' Toby said, recovering his poise. He rubbed his hands together. 'Well, well. Let's get down to business, then. You've brought the papers, have you?' His eyes fell on the briefcase in David's hand.

'Yes, Toby. They're in here.'

'Good. Well, let's get into them, David. Andrew is ready to go through them with you. You'll soon see how you've blown everything out of proportion, won't he, Andrew?'

'Too right, he will. Asleena, how about getting a drink for Miss Anders while we men do business?'

Before Asleena could respond, Sue waved her hand in refusal. 'No, thanks. I understand accountancy. I'd rather hear what you have to say, if you don't mind.'

It was clear that they did mind, but allowed it to pass. David got out both sets of papers and laid them side-by-side on the dining table. He began to point out some of the discrepancies he had found.

Sue stood behind him, feeling very apprehensive and alert for trouble, which she felt sure would come. There was no way Toby could satisfactorily explain away the discrepancies. Surely he must know that.

'David, David. Look. It's not what it seems,' Toby cajoled. 'What we've done isn't really illegal. There's been nothing more than a couple of imaginative exclusion ploys used to benefit our clients. It's what they pay us for, you know.'

He laughed with false bonhomie. 'You'll get your 'cut', of course. I was intending to promote you to full partnership after this year's returns had been dealt with satisfactorily. We can get the paperwork drawn up immediately, if you like. What d'you say, eh?'

David shook his head. 'I don't want anything to do with it, Toby. You must know that. You wouldn't have gone to so much trouble to keep me from seeing it all if you'd thought I'd go along with it.' He gave a short laugh. 'At least now I know why you didn't want anything to do with the proposed merger. Was that why you skipped abroad at this particular time? I thought it was a strange time to take a holiday.'

'And what do you suggest we do?'

Andrew asked coldly.

'Destroy all this, and start again with the correct details,' David said firmly. 'I'll help you sort it out. I'll work overtime. We can do it, Toby. Even with the office destroyed, you'll be able to start again.'

'And what do you think our clients will say about that?' Toby asked incredulously.

'I don't care what they say. They shouldn't expect you to lie on their behalf.'

'You're a fool, lad!' Andrew snapped. 'Why do you think they come to us? They don't pick out our name with a pin.'

'Us?' David queried. 'You are supposed to be an independent advisor.'

'A lot of people aren't what they are supposed to be.' Andrew sneered. He turned to Toby. 'I've had enough of this. We'll have to get rid of them, like we said.'

As he spoke, he whirled round and dug his elbow sharply into David's midriff, causing him to double over and stagger back into Sue. By the time Sue and David had recovered their balance, Andrew had them covered with a handgun.

12

Sue stared at the gun in disbelief. This couldn't really be happening. 'Sit down on those chairs!' Andrew snapped. 'I said, 'sit'!' he repeated, as they both hesitated. He waved the gun from one to the other. 'I will use it,' he warned. 'There's too much at stake to risk getting caught at this stage.'

Sue nervously dropped on to a dining chair, thankful to sit before her legs collapsed under her. David followed suit a bit more reluctantly.

Andrew looked towards Toby and Asleena. 'You two! There's a roll of tape in the bureau. Bind their wrists together with it. I've got them covered.'

'You don't think we came here without leaving word of where we were coming, do you?' David asked quietly, trying to keep the air calm. The way Andrew was waving the gun about, he feared it would go off with or without intention, and if he waited until their arms were fastened behind the chairs, they would have less chance of escape.

Andrew narrowed his eyes and looked at him scathingly. 'That's exactly what I do think. You came here to try to talk Toby out of the game and save the business. You won't have risked putting the firm in jeopardy.'

David shrugged, as coolly as he could with his arms being pulled back behind the chair by Toby. 'You're wrong. I sent a duplicate packet to my bank, with instructions to open it if I haven't telephoned by eight o'clock this evening. It contains copies of all those papers and back-up discs and a written explanation of all that has transpired, plus a note of this address. I'd say you have less than three hours to leave the country.'

'I don't believe you!'

'Then, more fool you!'

Andrew's eyes narrowed for a moment, and then he shrugged. 'No matter. You will telephone your bank and tell them that all is well.' He swiftly pointed the gun towards Sue. 'Otherwise, your little lady-friend will be blown out of existence.'

Sue's eyes widened in fear and she could see a flicker of indecision on David's face.

'Don't do it, David! He'll still kill us!'

She heard a swift intake of breath and realised that it came from Toby. His face was white with shock and he seemed to be looking from Asleena to Andrew in an attempt to fully take in what was happening. 'David, boy, it's not . . . er . . . too late to negotiate terms,' Toby attempted to bargain, letting go of David's arms and stepping to the side so that he could appeal directly face-to-face. 'We'll . . . er . . . tell our clients we can't continue, what with the fire and everything. We'll start a new business with the insurance money.'

He appealed to Andrew. 'We've had a good innings. Made a small fortune. We could call it a day, eh, Andrew?'

'I'll kill him first and risk it!' Andrew snarled, 'and you, too!' swinging the gun to point at Toby. 'I've not come this far to back out now just because a fresh-faced kid has scruples!'

'Now, look here, Andrew!' Toby protested, taking a step forward. 'We can't justify murder!'

'Can't we? What did you think was Asleena's intention when she ran them off the road? If you're not with me . . . '

David saw Andrew's intent in the stance he adopted and desperately lunged forward in a flying tackle, sending Andrew toppling to the floor. The gun went off but the bullet smashed into the wooden wall sending splinters cascading into the room as David and Andrew rolled over, each trying to gain the advantage.

Asleena screamed, her fingers spread across her face.

Sue had a sudden dread that she was about to lose David, just as she had lost all others whom she had dared to love.

'No!' she screamed. All she could think was that she wasn't going to lose David, not if she had anything to do with it!

With no thought to her own safety, she darted forward, kicked Andrew's hand that still clung to the gun and grabbed at the gun as it skittered across the wooden floor.

She had never held a gun before and didn't even know if it were still loaded. Nevertheless, she held it firmly and swiftly took in the situation.

David was kneeling on top of Andrew, who was now face down on the floor, and was holding Andrew's arms twisted across his back. Toby was still frozen in immobility with the shock of his close brush with death and Asleena was cringing behind him.

Her voice sounded stronger than she felt when she said, 'I think, Toby and Asleena, you had better sit down, on the floor, over there,' she added, pointing, remembering how David had been able to leap from his chair.

An inner door crashed open and the

agitated figure of the manservant rushed forward, pulling up in alarm at the sight of Andrew lying face down on the floor.

'Sir! Sir!' he cried. 'What is happening?'

He realised that Sue was holding a gun and he backed away with his hands in the air, even though Sue hadn't spoken a word. 'It's all right!' she now assured him. 'Go and phone the police.'

'The police? Mr Forbes? What shall I do?'

'Get him off me, you fool! Get him off me!' Andrew gasped.

'Leave him, Isam!' Toby intervened. 'Go back to your quarters! We'll sort it out.'

'Shall I phone the police, Mr Naughton?'

Simultaneously, Toby and Andrew said, 'No!' whilst Sue and David said, 'Yes!'

'Let's not be too hasty, David,' Toby suggested. 'I'm sure we can reach a compromise. What do you say?'

'I can't do anything whilst this fellow is still trying to get the better of me!' David grunted.

Toby reached out and rolled the tape towards David. 'Use that!' he suggested. 'I'll feel safer myself if he can't grab hold of that gun again. And do point it somewhere else, dear girl. I'm no more sure than you are whether it is still loaded or not!'

Sue grabbed hold of the tape and pulled out the free end. With David still restraining Andrew, she began to wrap the sticky tape round and round his wrists and then down his legs to his feet. It would take a lot of pulling to get it to tear apart.

David eased himself off Andrew's body and watched dispassionately as Andrew thrashed about for a few moments, until he admitted to himself that no amount of activity would tear the strong tape.

'You can sit up,' David told him, 'but don't try to stand.'

He turned to Toby. 'Right! What have

you to say, Toby? You'd better make it quick. I'm getting a bit tired of all this. It's been a trying day.'

'Let me go, David, lad,' Toby pleaded. 'You said we'd about three hours to leave the country. I could still make it. I'll go straight to the airport, I promise. I'll ring my wife and tell her where she can join me.'

'And what about me, you swine?' Asleena screeched. 'You said I was going away with you!'

Toby turned and carefully looked her up and down, distaste evident in his face. 'Sorry, Asleena. I wouldn't trust you.' He turned back to David. 'I never meant to kill you, lad. I just wanted you to keep your nose out of my files until I got back. Why did you have to be so keen to live and work by the book?'

David shrugged and smiled faintly, sadly almost, thinking of their now-severed partnership. 'It's the only way, in my thinking, Toby! I want to be able to face myself in the mirror every morning and . . . ' He put his arms around Sue and drew her close. ' . . . and face those I care about and love.'

Sue felt a thrill run through her, though she had known the truth of it all day. David loved her, and she loved him. It was meant to be. She lifted her face up to him and smiled into his eyes.

Toby had scrambled to his feet before either was aware of it and, after a moment's hesitation, so did Asleena. For all he had discarded her, she clung to his arm, wondering what he was about to do.

Sue lifted the gun again but Toby just smiled. 'You won't shoot me, neither to my face nor in my back, so I'm going to walk right out of here. I know you'll phone the police, but I might make it. There might be a plane going somewhere. I'll send you a postcard. So long!'

And, without a backward glance, he walked from the room and they heard his feet going down the wooden steps of the porch with Asleena's high heels tapping after him. Two car doors slammed and an engine started up, and the sound of it faded into the distance.

David looked over to where Isam still hovered indecisively by the inner door. 'Phone the police, Isam. And then, if I may, I'll phone my bank manager and a lawyer.'

He hugged Sue to him and smiled ruefully at her. 'It's going to be a long night!'

Three weeks later, David and Sue, along with Pastor Jacob, Bridget and all seventy-three boys and girls from The Sheepfold were guests at Amu and Vishnu's wedding.

The bride and groom, dressed in traditional kain songket, that is silk with gold thread, held out their hands whilst henna was applied to their palms and fingertips and then they *sat in state* on a dais under an arch of leaves and flowers to greet their guests, their friends, their families.

The couple were showered with flower petals called bunga rampai and thinly shredded pandanus leaves and were sprinkled with rose water as the guests offered a variety of modern and traditional gifts that were laid before them.

It had taken many days to prepare the feast. Aunt Rathi had rallied wonderfully once Vishnu arrived home from his spell of employment in the next state, proud to acknowledge his promotion, and magnanimous enough to wish them well in a home of their own.

When the guests moved on to the dancefloor, David stood in front of Sue, who was looking delightful in a pale blue dress that floated around her.

'May I have this dance?' he asked, his eyes twinkling with merriment.

He still couldn't believe how Sue had come into his life. The past three weeks had been fraught, as he had undergone many interviews by the police and tax inspectors. Andrew and Asleena were on remand for attempted murder, Toby had been apprehended in the departure lounge at Kuala Lumpur International airport and was awaiting his trial for submitting multiple fraudulent tax returns.

Sue had stood by him throughout it all, ready to cheer and to comfort him and finally to celebrate with him as he emerged with an unblemished professional reputation. It was over, and the rest of his life was about to begin.

'I'm enjoying this!' he whispered to Sue. 'I can't wait for the next one.'

'The next one?' Sue queried.

'Yours and mine!'

'Haven't you forgotten something?'

'No. I plan to do it later, when the air is balmy and quiet and I'll be able to make my request in a more romantic setting.'

'Request?'

'Proposal.'

'Ah!'

'What do you think she will say?'

'She?'

'The lady of my affections.'

'I think she'll say, 'Yes'.'